THE PARTY BUS

Samanvita Mangalampalli

INDIA • UK • USA

Copyright © Samanvita Mangalampalli, 2023

All rights reserved. No part of this publication may be reproduced, stored in a retrieval system, or transmitted in any form or by any means, electronic, mechanical, recording or otherwise, without the prior written permission of the author.

This book is a work of fiction. Names, characters, places, and incidents are either the author's imagination or are used fictitiously and any resemblance to any actual person living or dead, events and locales is entirely coincidental.

Paperback ISBN: 978-93-5574-446-3

Hardback ISBN: 978-93-5574-445-6

eBook ISBN: 978-93-5574-448-7

First Published in April 2023

Published by Walnut Publication
(an imprint of Vyusta Ventures LLP)
www.walnutpublication.com

USA

1820 Avenue M #849, Brooklyn, NY 11230

India

OU-625, Nexus Esplanade, Rasulgarh, Bhubaneswar – 751010

WeWork Berger Delhi One, Level-19, Sector 16B, Noida - 201301

THE PARTY BUS

PROLOGUE

In a still parking lot, in the dead of night, sat a bus. It lay silently among the other buses, like a great sleeping beast, joints creaking in the wind.

A man approached the bus. He ran a hand across its hood, caressing the muzzle of this familiar creature, and swiftly went inside. At the driver's seat, he crouched. From his pockets, he drew out a package. It was small, hard, and covered in plastic, and he didn't bother wearing gloves when he took it out and tucked it away safely in a cupholder in the door. It was mostly hidden by the driver's seat, only for the right person to find.

The man leaned back after he hid the package away, feeling short of breath as if he'd run a marathon. His heartbeat wildly. It was the only thing he could hear in the darkness. He wiped sweat from his brow, and proceeded to continue with his plan, fiddling with the dome of the bus's security camera. He knew the device didn't work anymore anyway. After he was done, the phones would work as well as the camera did. The man leaned back, minutes later, and took a second of silence to appreciate his work. Kharon, he'd called himself once. He was the psychopomp of Hades, but in the real world, he didn't exist. Not yet.

The man slipped off the bus, and walked away, leaving the bus laying there in the dark, waiting for its journey to begin.

ARMAND

The bus was pink.

It stood out in the parking lot at seven-thirty on that Saturday morning. It was a flamingo in a sea of white, gray, silver, and black of the other buses in the lot. The only writing on it was faded.

The man in the parking lot started walking towards it. His feet in faded leather loafers, his legs in desert-sand trousers instead of the typical navy-blue uniform. Upon his lapel gleamed not a badge, but a tiny emoji pins his niece had given to him a long while back. The yellow-faced circle had a colorful cone-hat on, and a party popper shoved into its mouth. Cheeks red, eyes closed. Alina had given it to him because 'every day is a party day'. She was six.

The man shuffled towards the pink bus. Its glowed neon in the light of the still-rising sun, comically intimidating, like a great big cartoon pig. Sitting in the front seat, his cigarette-wielding arm hanging out, was the driver.

"Hi," the man spoke. His toes twitched in their loafers. "Is this - is this bus actually public transport?"

The driver began to chuckle. He raised his cigarette to his lips, thought better of it, and went on to scratch his jaw instead. "Oh, yeah. I get that a lot. She's public transport, alright. Public bus. Just like all the others out here."

A little chuckle. "I guess you get that a lot, huh?"

"Oh, yeah. I guess that's on me. She's bright pink."

"I didn't know public buses could be any other color than white." "Well, here you go. They can."

"Yeah, I was standing right out there for a while. Didn't believe what I was seeing for a sec."

"Oh, yeah. I saw you. You need to go somewhere?" "Yeah. There's that art exhibit downtown…?"

"I think I've seen ads around." The driver raised his cigarette again, paused, then let his arm hang down again. This time, he let the little white stick slip from his fingers and disappear down the other side of the bus.

"Quitting?" The man noticed.

The driver nodded. "My wife thinks I've already quit. Don't tell her."

"I won't." The man looked around. "I guess I should wait at an actual bus stop now. I just wanted to say, that's an eye-catching bus you have there. That's it. Have a good day —"

"Well if you want, I can take you in it." the driver straightened. "Oh, no, no, that's fine, I —"

"I think it's on my route anyway —" "No, really —"

"My break is almost done anyway —"

Armand hesitated. The exhibition opened in half an hour. "Really? You sure?"

"Oh yeah. Hop on. I'll get you a ticket you can buy."

The driver reached through compartments and areas hidden by the pink of the bus, before pulling out a ticket and a pen. "Name?"

"Armand Ewing. That's a-r-m-a-n-d, e-w-i-n-g - Ewing."

His hand reached over from the window and held out the ticket. Armand's hand offered a five-dollar bill. A trade was made, with the sun, the empty buses, and pink as witnesses. The bus's door opened, and Armand got in.

The inside was not pink. It looked like a bus. Like any other bus. If one sat in it, on one of its hard seats, or stood near a pole holding one of the metal rungs, or stared outside the window, they wouldn't have ever known it was pink on the outside. Armand took a seat, placing his messenger bag next to him, and the bus started.

He inched closer and closer to the front until he could see the driver, then finally asked, "So what made you decide on pink?"

The driver didn't turn back, but he smiled. "I like the color. I dunno." "I see."

"It used to be a party bus once. Entertainment on wheels."

What happened? "I see."

The driver answered as though he could read minds. "You see some crazy stuff as a party bus driver. I decided I was too old for all that a while ago."

"That makes sense."

"I still see some crazy stuff. Public buses get all sorts." "I imagine they would."

Silence. Then the driver asked, "You like art?" "Huh?"

"You said you're going to the museum. The exhibit, the… uh, you know.

The art thing."

"Yeah. I'm okay with it."

"Meeting someone important, or…?"

"Not really." Armand smiled a little. "Just thought I'd try something out." "That's a fine way to live."

The driver turned back to his wheel, and Armand to the nearest window, watching regular, non-pink cars and bikes and buses and people scream by. The bus hit a light and stopped. Some people from the windows of other cars stared a bit. The light turned green, the bus took a left, and they continued in silence, and the occasional mild conversation, until the driver slowed to a halt near a bus stop. The bus doors opened, and a little elderly woman with a purse hobbled in.

"Ooh, what happened to the old one?" she asked, looking around. Her misty eyes stopped on Armand with disappointment. "I'm the first stop. I'm always the first stop."

"Sorry, ma'am." Armand mumbled.

The woman turned back to the driver. "What happened to the old one?

Where's the old bus?"

"Changed routes, ma'am," said the driver. The old woman muttered to herself, and finally sat, two seats behind the one across from Armand. The driver leaned back in his seat, watching the doors close. His gaze caught Armand, and he rolled his eyes. Armand smiled. He bit his smile away when he thought he saw the old woman glaring at him and fiddled with the straps of his bag. The bus started again.

ARMAND

The second stop was a lot closer to the first than the first was to the parking lot. It was tucked away on the side of the large road between two growing trees in fences, and this time, two of the waiting people got on. The first was a tall, slender woman, stunning to look at. Her hair was red-orange, cut neatly to her bony shoulders. Her pale skin was dotted with freckles—a natural redhead. She had on natural, minimal makeup, and casual clothes that fit her tall, well-proportioned body like a glove. She, too, upon entering the bus, looked at the driver, then Armand, with surprise.

"New bus?" she asked the old woman.

The old woman looked up at her and smiled, her face sinking into wrinkles.

"Oh, hi, dear. You look beautiful today."

The redhead sighed out a smile and spoke louder. "Hi, Evangeline. Is it a new bus?"

"Huh?" the old woman, Evangeline, asked.

The driver didn't look bothered to answer. As the woman inched into the bus on her thin ankles and heels, Armand answered quickly, "It's a new bus. The old one changed route."

The woman turned to him. "Oh. Thanks."

But her eyes stayed on him. On his face, his clothes, his hands, his bag, his shoes, and then his chest. She took the seat in front of him, sat sideways, and turned to face him. Her arm slid over the top of the seat, hanging casually.

"That's a nice brooch you have there," she said, pointing lazily.

"Thanks," said Armand. Up close, he thought, her face was even more beautiful. "My niece gave it to me."

As he talked, the woman looked away from him and down into her lap. Her face lit up light blue, and a tiny white light hit her brown eyes. She was looking at her phone. When he stopped talking, the light disappeared, and she looked again at him and smiled. "Oh, that's sweet."

As this took place, the second girl following the redhead had silently slipped into the bus and sat in the back. Her head was bent down, black hair falling around her ears and chin, but her eyes darted: to the left, at Armand, to the window, at Armand, at the old woman, at the driver, at Armand. She adjusted her glasses once, and looked back down at her phone. Armand resorted to staring out the window again. The bus droned on.

TAMANNA

There's a new bus today. It's bright pink. The driver is new too, and there's a new guy on it. The driver looks suspicious. Heavy build, tattoos on one arm, smells like smoke, has a beard. Evangeline doesn't like the new bus. I don't either. It feels weird getting on a bus and not going to school.

The girl put down her pen and sighed. Tamanna Raghavan always took the 42 routes to get to school. It was the fastest. She was the second stop going, the first stop coming back. The driver, Griffin, took shortcuts for her and made good conversation. The old driver did. The new one did what drivers were paid to do, and nothing else. The new bus —and the new color— threw her off more than anything else, but at least the usuals were still there. There was Evangeline, the oldie who needed everyone to know her opinions. She took the bus every day, regardless of whether it was a weekday or a weekend. Tamanna only knew her name because the model knew her name, and talked to her. Then of course, there was the model. Her name was something like Amy, and she spoke French with her friends on the phone a lot. She had contacts and important people to be with. She wasn't rich, though, because she took public transport. She had to be new to the industry.

Tamanna glanced up. She sat in the back of the bus, always, to deduce what she could from the people that sat there. Evangeline had been reading that book, the *Know Your True Value* book, for weeks and weeks now. She was always reading something about inner worth and true values and such. *Evangeline has been reading the same book for too long.* She was religious too, with the cross necklace around her sallow neck, that she clasped whenever she came across something particularly noteworthy in her books. *She touched her necklace four times without flipping the page.*

Tamanna's sloppy handwriting got sloppier towards the end of the sentence. Her wrist ached. She closed her diary and set it on her lap before glancing up. Where? She knew the scenery outside. She'd seen Evangeline before. The bus wasn't pink and interesting on the inside. The model was texting her boss again, but this time, every so often, she'd look up at the man sitting behind her, speak, and smile.

The man, the new guy, was sitting quietly behind the model. Did he get on before, or after her? Was he looking at her? Was he interested in her? Was that the way he always dressed -neat, proper, studious? What was in the bag on his lap?

Tamanna had glimpsed it secretly as she slipped away from half-deaf Evangeline, the ever-patient model, and the uninterested driver. Tamanna quickly opened her diary again. *Old bus route changed.* She closed it and looked back up. The neatly dressed man was staring at her. She looked down again. She wondered if she should have casually smiled instead of creepily staring and looking away.

The bus stopped again. A middle-aged man who Tamanna usually didn't see while going to school, entered the bus. He sat in one of the corner seats, blocking Tamanna's perfect view of the model and the neatly dressed guy. She didn't really know if he was a gym teacher, per se, but he wore those clothes — the sports jacket and matching track pants — and carried a neon-embroidered duffle bag and had that slightly unshaven discoloration around his cheeks and jaw that all gym teachers and trainers and coaches do. The gym teacher sat quietly and silently, a few seats in front of her, and faded into the background.

Then came a man in a cheap suit. He was good-looking and had pearly white teeth. Tamanna had never seen him before, either, and concluded that the weekend bus-takers had to be different. The cheap-suited man shuffled into an empty seat on the left side of the bus, thankfully blocking no one else from Tamanna's view, and hooked himself to his phone.

The last stop gifted three people to the bus: a young woman wearing a blue hijab, a blonde with an empty foldable stroller, and another quiet woman with earbuds and chains and jewelry hooked onto her the way tubes and wires hook onto a patient in the ER. The woman with the stroller stopped with a harsh, beaming smile, and said in a bubbly voice, "Ooh, this is a nice bus. What a fun color, huh?"

It was directed to no particular person, and so no particular person gave her an answer. She chuckled a little, then fumbled down the aisle with her metal stroller before sitting in the very back, close to Tamanna's seat. She caught Tamanna's glance and smiled. "My stop is far, far away," she said. "It's all the way to the DOT." Tamanna smiled and nodded. Department of Transportation. Did she work there? Did her spouse work there? Was she picking up her child?

The bus was in utter, awkward silence. All buses were, really. Tamanna felt like none of them -not even her- did the bright pink exterior of the bus any justice. *Maybe that's why buses are boring. The people inside mostly are. What are they, partiers?* Tamanna smiled a little to herself. *We're a party bus, in a party bus.* She found the woman with the stroller staring at her, and stopped smiling. She looked out the window. *Party bus, this is.*

The lights changed, the doors closed, and the party bus started to roll.

ARMAND

The bus didn't pick anyone else up. Armand counted a total of twenty-four tightly packed seats in the tiny bus, and only nine were being occupied. No two people sat together, and other than the beautiful redhead, no one seemed to know anyone else. Armand pulled out his phone. There was no service. For him and the limited plan being a police officer got him, at least; the redhead seemed to have no problem texting. Armand tucked his phone back into his messenger bag and looked out the window. They were nowhere close to downtown. They were nowhere close to the art exhibit, and the show started in fifteen minutes. Armand shuffled uncomfortably.

He turned around and found the girl's eyes staring at him again. The South Asian girl with the large glasses and the suspicious brown eyes. She'd changed her seat from directly behind him to the back seat of the row beside. The girl looked down again, and this time, Armand found what she had in her lap — not a phone, but a little square of brown diary that she scribbled furiously in. Was she tracking him?

Armand's first thought was to laugh. She wouldn't find much. Unless she found him being a police officer something to be excited about. Was she a junkie? She didn't look like one. Armand smiled to himself. Children. He remembered when he was around her age. Well, he didn't. Armand stared at her longer. He shifted in his seat, rested his arms on the back rest, and watched her. She looked up at him again, as she routinely did, and when she did, Armand smiled and waved. She blinked at him. Then, hesitating, she got up from her seat and hurried towards him as the bus rolled on.

"Can I?"

She pointed to the extension of his seat. Armand nodded, moved his bag into his lap, and scooched into the corner. She sat next to him. The girl was a reedy, slight, brown girl, with glasses and short black hair in a ponytail. She held a little bag and her diary. She looked over at him, thoroughly, absorbing whatever she could see, before stating simply, "Police."

Armand blinked. Behind them, the man in the sports tracksuit glanced up.

The pretty redhead, too, heard.

"How did you know?" Armand made sure to keep his voice low, to make her do the same.

The girl smiled. "I like Sherlock."

"Holmes, huh?" Armand smiled. "Your friends call you that?"

"Not really. They don't know." The girl looked down at the cover of her diary, fiddling. "I don't know why I told you that."

"I appreciated it anyway," Armand said. Silence. Then he asked, "What's your name?"

"Tamanna," The girl said.

"That's a pretty name. Indian?" Armand asked. Tamanna nodded. "What's your name?" She asked.

"Armand."

"Arabic or French?"

"Both. Half Egyptian."

"The other half?" Tamanna asked. She realized it after she asked, but he answered anyway. "French."

Tamanna nodded silently. Armand looked at her. She looked back, then cracked a smile. Armand returned it. The smiles turned into quiet chuckles.

Then a speaker crackled overhead. Armand, from his position close to the front doors, saw the driver lift a little remote on a curly wire up to his stiff beard. His lips moved, and from the speaker came his voice: "Ladies and gentle-people, there's a high amount of traffic at this current moment. We're taking a detour through the border of the acres of wildlife from the south to get downtown, because there's no way any of you are getting to your places on time through the main routes."

The man in the sports suit groaned a little. "C'mon, man, my students have a competition in a week."

"And my brother can't be trusted with little kids," the woman with the stroller said, with forced humor. "I need to get there before he eats them."

The silent girl with multiple piercings looked up from her phone. "So, you can eat them first?"

"What?" The woman with the stroller chuckled awkwardly.

The girl with the piercings smiled, revealing a row of brilliant white teeth, and two canines of silver and gold. "They're delicious."

"Satan's spawn," Evangeline said loudly, glaring up from her book. "Young people. Always going in a hurry, and never to God."

Armand's stomach flipped. Motion sickness. He turned to Tamanna, who sat quietly, flipping her diary open and shut.

"Where are you going?" "School," she answered.

"On a Saturday?" Armand asked, curious. Tamanna nodded. "I'm volunteering to clean up the gyms after sports practice on the weekends," she said. "Today's my first day doing it."

Armand nodded back. "You like volunteering? Helping people out?" Tamanna shrugged. "I get to meet a lot of new people. I don't really like going to school, but you know."

"You like to get all detective-y on them?" Armand chuckled. Only after Tamanna chuckled back did he continue and ask, "Don't you take a school bus? To school?"

Tamanna shrugged. "I don't like taking school buses. They get loud on the way back."

Armand nodded, and they lapsed into silence again. Outside the window, the scene turned from cars and buildings and slow traffic to trees and trees and more trees and green.

"How long will this route take?" The gym teacher asked again. Next to him, Armand realized for the first time, was a long, large gym duffel bag with the Nike logo. It leaned against the window, and crinkled when he placed a protective hand over it.

The driver lifted his radio speaker again. "Less time. That's all I can say, really. We're getting really winded up. Sorry, folks."

There was a round of groans throughout the bus, even from Tamanna. Then came a scream.

It was not a person's scream but a horrific, agonized screech from the wheels and engines of the pink bus. Something sputtered, exhausted, at the front of the bus. The vehicle halted.

"Folks, something's up with the engine." The driver's voice came again, even as the man stood from his seat. "I'll go check it out. Thanks for your patience." He exited the bus, and soon the pink of the bus's hood covered the scene from the front window.

The blonde woman huffed. The man in the sports suit groaned. "Come on, man." The redhead checked her watch and looked at her phone, again and again. Tamanna stuffed her diary in her bag and muttered, "I should just go home." Evangeline looked up from her book. "What's all the din?"

The redhead said loudly, "There's something wrong with the engine."

Evangeline looked around. "So? Can't we all appreciate this time we're getting to relax and settle in and look at the nature around us while Mr. Driver fixes it up? Always in a hurry. Young people, they're always in a hurry."

"We all haven't retired yet," Armand heard the sports coach behind him mutter. He twitched restlessly as the bus lapsed back into silence, and only the sounds of the driver tinkering around outside were heard. After a moment, he slung his bag over his shoulder and stood.

"Excuse me," he whispered to Tamanna. The girl stood and backed into the aisle. Armand shuffled to the open doors, and their little metal steps.

"Where are you going?" The redhead asked him. Was it just him, or did she sound worried?

"Oh, just to see if I can help out at all." Armand gestured to the open hood through the bus's window. The redhead nodded, and turned her phone back on. Tamanna, instead of returning to the back, sat in Armand's seat and patiently waited for him. Armand hopped off the bus.

ARMAND

The organs of the great pink beast were steaming. It squealed at the touch and cried great big tears of pain that leaked around its wheels, its stocky legs, in the form of some strong-smelling liquid. The driver leaned over it, scratching his head. His fingers trembled, and Armand knew they were simply itching to hold another cigarette, even if he wouldn't smoke it.

"Hey." Armand dropped his bag near the only dry wheel and walked around the hood. "Need help?"

The driver looked up at him and sighed. "I'd say yes, but I'm not too sure what happened either. Guess I shouldn't have made my thirty-year-old party bus public transport, huh?"

"That could possibly be it," Armand said awkwardly. "They're getting restless in there."

The driver glanced up at the front window as if he could see the bus inside from it. "Well, they're going to have to be restless a little patiently." Armand cracked a smile. "So, what are you going to do?"

The driver shrugged. His hand raised to his face, hesitated near his mouth, then ran its fingers through his balding hair. "I'm not sure. I know the route to downtown. I could run up there and ask for help."

"If it isn't too far away, yeah." Armand pulled out his phone. "Is this a good instance to call emergency services?"

The driver slapped his forehead with his palm. It made a harsh, abrupt noise that sounded very different from the bus's drawls and dying moans. "Oh, yeah.

Why didn't I think of that?" He patted his pockets around. "I forgot my phone on the bus."

"I have my phone," Armand said quickly. He pulled it out. "There's no service, though. I've never been in a bus with such awful…" he glanced at the driver. "No offense."

The man shrugged. "I don't know what to tell you, man. It sucks."

Armand shook his head. "But I'd assume you don't need service to make emergency calls…"

He pulled out the phone app and began to type in a number—a good friend of his in the towing services. 5. 4. 9—

Something slammed into him from behind. Armand stumbled forward. The phone tumbled from his hand to the ground, something cold and wet seeped down his jacket and the back of his neck, and the ground got closer and closer and closer and closer and—Armand toppled. When he recovered, some shaky moments later, he struggled to his hand and his knees.

The gym coach stood behind him, eyes wide. He had a bottle of Gatorade in his hand, now half empty. The other half was sticking to Armand's best clothes, and frying his phone. Armand grabbed the phone and checked it. It was gone. It had died, like the great pink beast's engines.

"That was five hundred dollars," Armand whispered. He sat there on his knees, the wet phone in his palms. The coach gently capped his bottle.

"Hey, man, sorry," he started. "I wanted to come out and help, but there was this thick-ass bag in the way, right here—" he pointed to Armand's bag leaning against the wheel. "Is it dead?"

It took Armand a moment to understand. He lifted the wet phone. "Yeah."

"Oh, man. Sorry." The coach scratched his head. "Sorry about your suit, too. I have a spare tracksuit, if you want. One of my students is always forgetting hers."

"It's okay, really." Armand gritted his teeth. "No, really—"

"I don't really need—"

"Mister, you'd better take it," The driver said. He had left his spot at the hood to stand behind Armand. "We're not going anywhere any time soon, and Gatorade, if you can tell, is different from water."

Armand accepted the clothes with a sigh. The coach produced a black tracksuit with neon orange and green stripes along the sides. Only after he accepted it did Armand realize he didn't have a place to change. And so, under the watch of the driver, he took tissues from the bus's glove compartment and hid himself behind a thick stack of trees down the side of the road. He wiped the Gatorade off and donned his new attire. He wanted nothing more than to go home, and forget about the exhibit. *Try something new, they said. Every day is a new day.*

Grumbling and grouching to himself, Armand wadded up the remains of his fine trouser and jacket and plucked his way through shrubs back to the glaringly pink bus.

First, he heard the voices.

They were agitated. Multiple voices, voices that had barely spoken on the bus, agitated and loud and confused and worried. Armand returned to the roadside from the trees. The members of the bus —nine in total, with him— stood outside the bus. The woman with the stroller held her metal shield with one hand, the other flying to her forehead, from her forehead, to her side, from her side, to her face.

Evangeline finally had her book, *Know Your True Value*, back in her large purse, looking confused and annoyed, asking from time to time, "Huh?" and "What did he say?" and "What did she say?" and the redhead scratched her red hair and whispered urgently. The gym coach seemed to be explaining something, looking as if he did not understand what he was saying.

Armand ran. His first instinct, and his first action, was to grab his bag that lay by the wheel, suffocating between people's feet. Only then did he turn to Tamanna and ask, "What happened? What's got everyone like this?"

Tamanna had to be asked twice. "The driver," she said finally, turning to him. Her eyes were brown and small and thickly lashed. "He left."

An image of the driver and his beard, his hanging cigarette, and his twitching mouth flashed across Armand's face. "What do you mean, *he's gone?*

Gone?"

Tamanna nodded. Her face was sunken in worry. "He's gone. He left us.

Why did he leave us? Did he do this on purpose, did he plan an ambush? Are they going to kill us, are they-"?

"We're going to be fine." Armand turned away from her, and shouldered his way to the gym coach—wearing the man's loose clothes. "What's going on here? Where's the driver?"

"He told me he was going to get help," the man said. "I told him not to, obviously, because he's the only person here who knows where we are. The only goddamn person who actually knows where we are, and I told him not to go anywhere, that we could get another phone."

"His phone was in the glove compartment, in the bus." Armand couldn't remember if he had seen it while getting himself tissues.

The coach only shook his head. "Nope. He checked. Turns out he forgot it at some gas station or something. It's gone." "What about yours?"

The coach snorted. "I don't *own* a cell phone. I've got a handy landline, I can do maths in my head, and if I need to play games, I get out my trusty bow. I shoot my entertainment, not tinker with a little bright box."

Armand gritted his teeth. "Someone must have a phone. That woman? I saw her with it a while ago. Two of them had phones. I know."

"We didn't get there yet." the gym coach gestured to the people out there. "They're still shocked at the driver being gone."

Armand prepared to search for the redhead, and demand her phone. The image of it flashed through his head, surely—the pale face lighting up blue, darkening her freckles to gray, the tiny lightbulbs of the screen twinkling in her brown eyes, and the twitch of a smile as a reaction to whatever the gadget showed her. She had a phone. She had one. But before he could march up to the woman, someone blocked him.

Armand looked up and up, into the eyes of a man wearing a suit. He wore a flashy tie, and a smile that showed two rows of straight teeth. "Is that really necessary?" The man asked. His voice was smooth and persuasive.

"What do you mean?"

The man shrugged. "I mean, our driver doesn't mean us harm, or at least, it doesn't seem like it. I came out to help just as he was saying that stuff about getting help. He was real convincing. I have a phone with me right now, see?" —he pulled out a black cellphone— "I say we wait, for ten, fifteen minutes. Maybe even twenty, thirty. If our driver doesn't return with help and gas and whatever else he needs to get this pink thing going, we can call the police."

Armand blinked. It was a slow, steady realization, as though he had stopped everything he was doing, and finally took the time to hear the birds singing in the sky. He didn't have a reason to panic and call his friend. Wasn't the driver a good person? He'd ended his break early and added a stop to his route to accommodate Armand. He made conversation. He was humane.

"You're right," Armand said finally. "Let's wait this out and see."

"That's more like it."

Armand felt a heavy hand on his back, and with it a little sting that shivered down his spine. The charming man's blue eyes—hauntingly blue eyes that every blue-eyed person seemed to have—bored into him, pale and stark against his dark skin, and suddenly, Armand felt uncomfortable, though he'd entirely forgotten about the Gatorade remains licking his skin.

"Can you help me calm them all down?" Armand asked finally. He stood with the man near the smoking hood of the bus, and stared out at the hysterical woman with the stroller and the deceptively calm redhead and the quietly panicking woman with the piercings. "Or at least, some of them?"

"Of course, man." The man in the suit turned away from the others and to him. He stuck out a large, bare hand. It contained no rings, no watches, no freckles or wrinkles or scars, only hair. "I'm George. Nice to meet you, though not in this circumstance."

Armand reached out. His hand was swallowed by George's smooth, pale hand, suffocated, squeezed, and shaken, before it was released. "I'm Armand. Nice to meet you too. Now let's get to it, eh?"

George nodded and walked off, straight to the loudest person there - Evangeline. He started to talk to her in low, comforting tones. Armand only heard fragments of the placating dialogues: "What's your name… Evangeline? That's a great name… Christian, huh? It sounded biblical… Well, see here…"

His voice flowed softly, like a little stream trickling over rocks, slowly shaping and warping them to something smooth and curving and cold. As Armand walked past him, he saw just the glint of something in those blue eyes—a sharp glint, filled with hidden annoyance, crippling anger, and restrained, veiled abuse. Armand nearly stopped walking in surprise. He stood there, shocked, for a second, before George's voice, still comforting as ever, reached his ears again: "So I really do think that's a good idea… trust me with it."

But Armand couldn't shake off the look in that man's eyes — something ready to inflict pain, something thin and stretched out and strained to the point of snapping, and when he snapped, terrible things would happen. Something so sinister even as his voice soothed and seduced like the Sirens. Armand worked his jaw, then whirled around to face George.

Someone screamed behind him.

This time, it was a human scream. It rang out, then dissolved into sobs and cries of "oh my god, oh my god!"

The voice belonged to the woman with the stroller. Only now, the metal and plastic carrier she'd been carrying around as if it really contained an infant was thrown to the ground, forgotten. She walked, trembling, around the back of the bus. Her hands flew to her mouth, her jaw was dropped, her eyes wide and red with horror and tears. "Oh my god, oh my god, oh my god —"

"What happened?" Armand ran to her. In a flash, there were people around her, comforting her. The tall girl in the hijab was rubbing her shoulders, and the redhead had a hand on her back. "Are you okay? What happened?"

The woman sobbed. "We-we hit something. We hit a rabbit. We killed the rabbit." She pointed to the back of the bus. "Back there — it's dead."

Armand found himself walking. He rounded the back of the bus, and sure enough, close to the wheels, was the little, lifeless body of a rabbit. It couldn't have been bigger than his forearm, and it was white and black — now white and black and red — all over. Its limbs were crushed, most likely from being run over.

"How did that happen?" Armand talked to himself, rather than anyone else.

The rabbit, the tire tracks, and the edge of the pink bus and its lights filled his view, but he still saw those accusing, angry blue eyes. "The bus didn't bump. We could have hit it, but we didn't run it over. We didn't run it over."

There was no one to answer his question. There was no one next to him, and no little voice in his brain. Armand straightened, and returned to the group of people. Nearly half of the nine people had gone back inside the bus—the crying woman and her entourage. She sat sniffling in one of the seats, no longer crying, but hugging the handle of her stroller and wiping her puffy eyes with a tissue.

When Armand entered the bus, and she saw him, she straightened herself out and sniffled away what she could of her tears.

"I'm sorry I got like that," She said quietly. Armand sat in the seat in front of hers, and turned to face her fully. "I just—I have trauma."

Before he could find a way to ask politely, she answered. "We used to have a dog, back when I was a little girl. He was a white lab. Barnacles. He was my best friend. Then one day, when I was six—or maybe seven—he went missing, and I found him three days later. He'd been run over or-or something, I don't know, but his face was all red and crushed and… it was just awful. I don't know what happened to him, but just seeing that little white rabbit turned all red, just like my poor dog, I just-I couldn't take it. I'm sorry."

"It's okay," the girl with the headscarf said softly. "Theresia, look at me. It's okay. It wasn't your fault, it was the driver's, if it was anyone's fault at all. It was an accident. And you were just sitting in the bus. You had nothing to do with it."

"I know but I just..." The woman, Theresia, said. Her voice wavered and broke. "That rabbit was white, too, and all I could think of was my poor Barnacles."

"It's okay, really," said Armand. He stayed for a moment longer. Behind the little group, the redhead stood hunched over at the very back of the bus. She stared out the rear window silently, her phone trembling in her hand. Armand watched her for a second, watched Theresia sniffle a moment longer, then got up and went out of the bus. The girl with the piercings was walking around the bus, from the back, presumably after seeing the rabbit. She looked at him passively, then over at George, who was talking to the gym coach quietly. She stared, something gleeful flashing in her small black eyes. Her lips, painted brown and red, twitched in a smile. Then she got on the bus.

Armand shivered, and tore his gaze away from the open doors the girl had gone through, back to George. The gym coach was describing Theresia's state. Armand wanted to join them. He wanted to ask George something, anything. He wanted to see that glint in George's eyes again, just to make sure he wasn't dreaming, just to know it had been there. Instead, Armand walked back behind the bus, to see the rabbit's corpse.

It was gone.

Armand stumbled to the sides of the roads, where the trees and shrubs of the forest started in an uneven line. There was no body thrown aside, no white fur traces stuck between the grass blades. There was only a little blood stain behind the bus, where it once was. The rabbit was gone.

AMES

S he'd seen it all.

Ames Perrault was a model. She'd always been one. Since she was four, she'd been a child model, and since she was twelve, she'd been a teen magazine model, and since she was eighteen, she'd been a brand model. The world of modeling was cutthroat and toxic, and she'd done terrible things. She'd seen terrible things.

But nothing she had ever seen had ruined her as much as the girl on the pink bus.

There had come a cry from the rear end of the bus. Theresia, the poor young mother, had seen a dead rabbit. She had gone in, shaking and crying and revealing to people the truth of her past with her family dog, and Ames had gone in with her. Theresia took a seat in the front, and people crowded around her.

Ames's phone buzzed. It buzzed every five minutes. She pulled it out of her pocket. On the lockscreen was a notification.

Sheila: I got you the part.

Sheila: They'll make it official when you get to work today. Sheila: Waiting for you.

Sheila: Please

Ames tried not to smile. Those men in the front, for a while, had come around, asking loudly for phones to call the police. Ames had not been asked yet by the time they stopped, but if she had been, she would have refused. She didn't want to endure the risk of someone seeing her messages, if Sheila sent the wrong text at the wrong time.

Ames shuffled to the back of the bus, and settled against the rear window. One of her friends responded to her most recent Instagram post: *la plus belle <3.* Another colleague contacted her after two weeks: *Been a while. Drinks?* Sheila sent another message: *Please come to work. I promise. Please. Or I can ask them to give it to me and send it to you. At least promise.*

Sheila: Please

Sheila: Please delete the pictures. Sheila: I promise it's done.

Sheila: Please

Ames's fingers twitched. She thought of how to respond. She stared at the screen for several seconds, imagining how it would look if it were in real life - Sheila begging, tears pooling at the corners of her perennially lined eyes, promising to do whatever. Ames hated it. She loved it and she hated that she loves it.

Movement caught her eye from outside the bus. Ames remembered only then, that right outside was the corpse of the rabbit. Apparently, they'd run the creature over. She hadn't felt it at all when they were driving.

The woman with the witch-like taste in appearance stood over the rabbit, staring at it. Ames watched her from the window. She looked down on the corpse like the goddess of death staring down at her skeleton army. She shifted on her foot in its leather coated boots with their laces and chains. She squatted, and touched the rabbit's body. Ames recoiled, but no matter how much she tried, she felt incapable of looking away. From her little spot on the other side of the stained, murky bus window, she watched the woman — her name was Eden, like the garden, she recalled — lift the corpse gently, as if to give it a burial, or make it a sacrifice.

She pulled out a little silver pocket knife, Lifted the rabbit's ear with a finger, Then, she tore it off.

She wiped it off on her shirt,

And she washed it well with a little bottle cap of water from a container in her backpack,

And then, she ate it. Ames watched her.

Then the woman made a face of distaste, but she chewed it and chewed it and swallowed it. Ames sat there on the bus, not moving, not speaking, as the young man with the emoji brooch entered the bus, asked Theresia questions, then left. With each footstep of his down the three metal steps under the door, Eden tore, cleaned, and ate another piece of the critter. When the man's feet thudded on the crumbling road, she wiped her mouth neatly. She collected the small, stained bones of the rabbit, cleaned of its meat, stored them in her bag, leaving behind only the blood soaked into the dirt, and stood. Then she froze.

She turned her head up, through the window, through the glass stained with fingerprints, and looked into Ames's eyes.

Eden smiled.

Ames drew herself away from the window, shivering. *What did I see? What did I see? What did I just see?*

She didn't see a woman eat a rabbit's corpse. She didn't see it.

Ames looked at her phone again. Sheila had sent four new messages:

Sheila: Please, I'm begging you.

Sheila: Are you there?

Sheila: Please respond, please tell me it's over.

Sheila: I won't tell the police, I swear.

Ames did not respond. She only tucked her phone into her purse, and left the bus. The man who seemed to be in control of it all, the man with the cool head, stood out, arms crossed. His name was George. He was talking seriously with the man with the pin—Armand—and the man in the tracksuit. Ames walked to them, tucking her trembling hands into the pockets of her trench-coat. Tears whelmed her eyes, and she blinked them away.

"Excuse me, boys."

Usually it worked with ease. Now she could barely whisper. But whisper it she did, whatever she could to get their attention. "I'd hate to interrupt this, or leave at a time like this, but a woman has some needs too." She gestured towards the forest easily, as though she was not screaming and crying and agonized and terrified on the inside. Armand and George exchanged quick glances with each other, before the first man's eyes widened a fraction. Armand nodded. "You don't need to ask or anything. We're not in charge."

George's lips twitched. Ames answered, still whispering, "Of course not.

I'm just making sure someone knows. I wouldn't want anyone to go missing looking for me, eh?"

"Oh. Right." Armand smiled at her. "As long as you don't run away."

Ames looked him full in the eye. His hazel eyes stared right back, uncertain and human. "I," she said, "Would never, never run away. I am not running away."

The man seemed a little taken aback. Ames didn't care. She shoved her hands deeper into her pocket, but instinct pulled them back out. Without thinking, she touched the pin on his chest. It was the partying emoji.

He looked down at it fondly. "My niece says every day's a party day." He smiled wistfully. "Party day, huh?"

Ames smiled, and this time it was harder to hide her tears. She drew herself away, put her hands back in her pocket, and walked to the side of the road, and into the bushes. She walked and she walked, and then she ran.

Ames Perrault stopped only to take off her high heels. She ran as fast as her legs would take her. And yet, she heard footsteps behind her. Someone was following her. *Run,* she told herself. She knew that if she didn't, she would die.

She would die if she stopped, and let Eden catch up to her. And so, she ran faster. Then she thought of Sheila, and her texts: *Please. Please. I'm begging you. Please.*

Ames stopped. She pulled out her phone. She sat there, against the bark of a moss-covered tree, went to her photo gallery, and deleted every single picture on her camera roll. Then she texted Sheila: *I've deleted them.*

I'm so sorry.

The footsteps crashed into the bushes before her. Eden appeared, running after her with all her might like a starving predator, desperate for its next meal. Ames couldn't run. She didn't want to. She was no longer Ames— she was Sheila now, being hunted and haunted by someone who soullessly preyed and laughed. She couldn't go on the way Sheila had. She couldn't hold on.

"You know it has to be like this," Eden whispered, panting.

"Make it quick. Please," Ames murmured. "Make it quick and kill me, or I'll run —and you know I can outrun you— and I'll tell everyone what I saw." Eden advanced. "And what did you see?" She asked sweetly.

"You eating that rabbit's body," Ames said. The images of it flashed in her head. "I saw you eating it."

Eden crouched before her. The girl had brown eyes, but she wore white lenses over them. Her hair was brown, dyed red. Her fake lashes fluttered. "That was the first time anyone's seen me eat." Her eyes scanned Ames hungrily, then gazed out at the empty trees and bushes around them. "It won't happen this time."

Ames realized what she meant. And suddenly, she didn't want to die. The horror of Eden's truth dawned upon her like a terrible, slow eclipse, and Ames could not believe she had stopped running.

"Make it quick. Make it quick," she whispered.

Eden pulled out a sleek pocket knife. Her eyes fell to the phone in Ames's hands. "I've seen you text the entire ride."

"Make it quick," Ames whispered. "I wonder who you keep texting." "Make it quick and kill me."

"Is that what's making you all suicidal?" "Make it quick!"

Eden smiled, and held the knife to Ames's throat. Cold, sharp metal touched the model's neck. "Yes, ma'am. I'll figure it all out when you're gone anyway."

Gone. Not dead, gone. Ames closed her eyes. Her life didn't flash before her eyes. Not her text messages, not the pictures she took, not the memory of taking the pictures, not her family, not her career, nothing. Nothing.

Ames Perrault had no last thoughts when she died.

ARMAND

Half an hour later, there was no driver, and people started to get hungry. It was Evangeline first, of course, who brought up food when they were all pressed and waiting for the driver to return. Theresia had stopped crying a long time ago. She now stood with her hands on her hips, periodically conversing with the gym coach, whom she addressed as Walter. They stood outside, near the dead engine that had long since stopped steaming. Tamanna had turned from shocked to exhausted, and resorted to playing offline video games on her phone in the bus. George stood off to the side, alone and silent. The hijabi woman sat inside, reading the book Evangeline had kindly offered to her. Ten minutes ago, the woman with the multiple piercings —Eden, her name was— had gone off to relieve herself. The redhead still had not returned.

Evangeline started. "Does anyone have food around here? No point in starving ourselves while we wait."

There was a round of mutters of "I don't have anything" and "I'm hungry too" all around, but the food was absent.

"We need to be alive for them to rescue us," Evangeline said loudly. "If Mr Driver's going to rescue us at all."

She had a fair point. Armand looked around. "Anyone have anything? Snacks?" He turned to Walter. "You had Gatorade with you. Have any more?"

Walter turned red, probably with the memory of the little accident that had led to the death of Armand's phone. "I..." he sighed. "I think I do. My students need protein, so I usually get some protein snacks with me to give them..."

"Protein!" Evangeline scoffed. "Even better, we can sustain ourselves."

Walter returned to the bus. He reappeared a moment later, his long archery bag in his arms, Tamanna and the hijabi girl following. From there, he opened his bag and the coach began to distribute what he had with him: protein bars, shakes, energy drinks, cereal bars, and chips. The heavy protein bars were given to the hungriest, and Armand instinctively lied, saying he wasn't really hungry, and so a solitary vitamin gummy and a mini packet of Doritos were the only things slapped into his palm. He popped in the gummy and walked over to the hijabi girl, who leaned against the wall, a small chocolate protein shakes in her hand, book in the other. *Know Your True Worth,* read the cover.

"Evangeline's real nice," he started, pointing to her book. "If that isn't your own copy, of course. Is it good?"

The girl looked over at him. The top of her smooth lip was coated with a thin moustache of milk. Armand smiled as disarmingly as he could manage. "I'm Armand."

"Ilays."

"That's a nice name.""Thanks."

Armand pointed to her book again. "*Know Your True Worth.* Is it good?"

The girl stared at the book as though she'd never seen it before. "Yeah. It's a bit deceiving, though."

"How is it deceiving?"

"You'd think it'd be about self-esteem, confidence, things like that. But no.

It's literally about your true value—organs, their worth and their value based on your health."

"Why would a sweet old lady read about that?" Armand cracked a smile.

"Was little Miss Evangeline a coroner back in her day?"

Ilays shrugged, slowly returning the smile. "I don't know." "You didn't ask?"

"Well, I did. The thing is, she's old. Was in an elderly home for a while, for dementia. She doesn't remember a thing from her younger days."

"Aw. That sucks."

Armand lingered a moment, then walked away. Tamanna had with her a peanut-butter protein bar, being the young, runty teenager of the bunch. Her brows were still creased with worry and annoyance, and now, there were dark circles under her eyes.

"Hey."

The girl looked up, and her tightly knit eyebrows unravelled slightly. "Hey.

You didn't get much."

Armand held up his Dorito packet. "I'm not too hungry anyway." The lie slipped easily between his teeth again. "So, hey. You like Sherlock Holmes, right?" "Yeah…"

The tight lines appeared on her forehead again. Armand leaned over. "I have a mystery for you."

The annoyance turned to curiosity.

"So Ilays, over there-" Armand pointed with his chin, "got that book Evangeline was reading. You know Evangeline, right?"

"Oh yeah, she's on the usual route with me all the time. Always reading those self-worth books, touching her necklace all religiously."

"Yeah, her. Turns out those books she's reading on self-worth —or least, just this one— aren't metaphorical. They're about *actual* self-worth. How much your organs cost, and all."

Tamanna's eyes went wide. She snickered faintly in surprise. "What's that old geezer planning?"

Armand shrugged. "Me, I thought she might have been a coroner back in the day, or something of the sort."

"Did you ask her?"

Armand bit back a smile. "Ilays did. Evangeline has dementia, apparently."

Tamanna's dark eyes gleamed with childish madness. "And so, the plot thickens. Say no more." She walked away with so much purpose that it was fascinating to watch.

That was when Eden returned.

The girl was wide-eyed. Through her drawn-on eyebrows and her white lenses and her pale-powdered face, she was worried. Scared, even. She marched over to them and said loudly, "Hasn't she returned yet?"

"Who?" Theresia asked. Others looked around and wondered, but immediately, Armand knew who. The redhead.

"She said she was going to relieve herself," he murmured.

Eden huffed. "I went too. Then I went looking for her. She's gone. I can't find her."

"What do you mean, you can't find her?" Walter snapped. "Where could she have gone?"

"I don't know —" Eden cut herself short, wide-eyed. "What if —"

"What if *what*?" Armand snapped, stepping forward. His heart tripped over its own heartbeats. Images of her face, lit up by her screen, and images of the dead rabbit -covered in blood, mottled white and black-flashed through his mind.

George's blue eyes glared at him.

"She kept looking at her phone," Eden whispered. "She kept looking and smiling. In relief. She had contact with the outside world."

The outside world. As if they were trapped on a different planet, or in a cave hundreds of miles below. They were out of fuel, on a compact little pink bus, stuck on a road somewhere between the trees of the woods. But it really felt like they'd been trapped on Mars, their space capsule, the only way back to Earth, broken and out of gas, their pilot, the driver, gone.

"What are you trying to say?" George asked finally. Armand nearly jumped.

He'd appeared as if out of nowhere, right at Eden's shoulder. "What are you insinuating?"

"She got help." Eden's voice was calm and quiet, and pale with realisation. "She ran away. She escaped. She abandoned us."

"Abandon?" Ilays scoffed meekly. "We're not chummy, we're not best friends. She was some bus rider that couldn't take the stress of being late to her photo shoot. Sure, it was selfish that she couldn't take us with her, but it's dumb if anyone here actually expected her to help at all."

George nodded. "She's absolutely right. So what if one person's gone? If Ames abandoned us, she'll have her justice. As long as the rest of us stick together until the driver comes back, or until someone comes our way, or whatever we can do to get back to civilization, it'll be okay. Ames leaving won't take us down — if she even left at all. It shouldn't."

The redhead — Ames — was gone. It was difficult, but not so difficult to

consider the possibility that she'd gotten help and abandoned them. Armand didn't realize at first how easily they'd skipped past the possibility that she was lost, out there in the woods somewhere. A friend could have picked her up. Her assistant, her manager. A crumbling pink bus full of random strangers wasn't worth helping to a fashion model.

"Look, there's nothing we can do about it now," George continued. "Ames has it coming for her. She'll get what she deserves. Let's just focus on us now.

Let's stick together from now on. Got it?"

No one said anything, but the promise was made. It hovered in the air, hanging with burden, unwilling to exist, but it existed nonetheless, as an invisible oath. They would stick together.

They dispersed, slowly, exhaustedly. Armand stared at the backs of the people he had only met that morning, yet had already spent a lifetime with.

"It's been nearly an hour since we got stuck here," Walter was saying quietly to George as they began to walk away. Ilays, Tamanna and Theresia returned to the safe insides of the bus. Evangeline began a brisk pace, back and forth along the length of the bus, to 'keep her cholesterol levels down'. Walter and George continued to converse by the open hood at the front of the unconscious pink beast. Eden walked along the roadside, hands shoved in her pockets. Her long, white, woollen scarf fluttered behind her as she paced.

The hem of the scarf was stained red.

ARMAND

A rmand looked around, then up at the sky. It had been an hour since the driver left. The art exhibit must have already started, and been well under way. Tamanna's classmates must have already finished cleaning up without her. Ilays must have finished her book about organs. Ames could have already arrived and begun her photo shoot. And it was hardly nine in the morning.

Armand decided to walk about for a bit. The thought of getting back on to the bus, and sitting on those hard leather seats brought about a wave of regurgitation. So, he too, like the elderly Evangeline, began to walk back and forth. First in the middle of the road, to keep up with Walter and George's conversation, but when he found nothing important to eavesdrop on, he moved to the side of the road, close to the trees. He remembered Ames's shining brown eyes, suddenly wet, and her polished hand touching his pin. *Every day's a party day.* To Ames, it certainly was.

Armand walked. He walked and he thought. That was all he did, for a good ten minutes, until he was sure the official hour had passed.

When he decided to return to the bus, he saw it.

Something gleamed between two sprouts of bushes. Something small and black, that reflected the light of the sun. The corner of the phone case had a dark reddish-brown stain. Armand walked back to it, crouched before the bushes, and took it in his hands. The black rectangle turned into an image—a professionally taken picture of a red-haired woman, with the time over it. 9:06 am.

Armand shot to his feet and held it up, to George and Walter, to Eden, to Evangeline, to the bus. "Ames's phone! I found Ames's phone!"

Eden's head snapped up. George and Walter turned around with surprise. Armand raced straight to the bus and up the three metal steps. "I found Ames's phone, lying in the bushes."

Walter stuck his head through the doors and within the minute, everyone was standing outside and around Armand, staring at the phone in his hand.

"Maybe she forgot it behind?" Eden offered.

"That doesn't make sense," Tamanna said. "If she called someone to make them pick her up, it isn't likely she'd forget it, that too. Where did you say it was?"

Armand pointed. There really was no way she left it behind.

"So, she could be lost—" he started to suggest. And then he remembered. He remembered Ames's hands in her pockets, walking towards them insecurely, her ankles trembling in her red heels, her face twitching, but most of all, he remembered her words, before she'd touched the pin he'd stapled to his tracksuit: *I would never, never run away. I am not running away.*

She wasn't lost. She wouldn't abandon them. And she hadn't run away.

Armand looked up at the people around them. "Does anyone know her password? Does anyone know how to get into phones?"

TAMANNA

The password was 7-4-3-4-5-2. Tamanna had seen the model type it in, over and over again. She seized the phone, entered in the numbers, and returned it to Armand. The man took it, surprised, and held it in his hand —a hidden universe of a model's world — before the classy businessman, George, took it from him.

"People," he started, in that annoying, persuasive voice. "What do we even have to gain from this, huh? Why are we out here looking through a girl's phone instead of going out to search for her, or just staying here and keeping ourselves safe? We're all tired and impatient, yes. But we're not hungry anymore. We're not thirsty. We have a place to sleep and shelter if it rains. We have company, we have each other. We haven't lost our sanity yet, and we certainly haven't lost our humanity yet. I don't think we should do this. It isn't right."

Tamanna felt Theresia twitch beside her. There was heavy breathing. An inhale, an exhale, and inhale, and exhale, and another inhale. Before the next exhale, there was a low growl, and Eden stumbled forward wildly. "Give me that!" George held it out of his reach, staggering backwards. "What-"

He didn't have time to finish. The convincing, honey-dripping man, the pinnacle of comfort, the silver-tongued snake-charmer was at a loss for words. They all watched Eden wildly scroll through the phone. "That little model. That little perfect model," she hissed to herself, her finger flying. "Perfect model with nothing to hide. Didn't abandon us. Of course not. She's beautiful. She's beautiful and perfect."

George blinked, wide-eyed, stiff. Those blue eyes of his did not disappear under his eyelids for a single second. They were hollow and confused and displaced. Walter snatched the phone from Eden and held it out of her reach.

"What are you *doing?* What are you looking for?"

Eden scowled. "There'll be something in her phone, something on her apps, that'll tell us where she is."

"Then why—" Walter scoffed. "What are you mumbling about? Beautiful?

Perfect? Secrets —what *secrets?*"

Eden scowled harder. The girl's sharp, drawn eyebrows turned inward. The darkly colored lips turned down. Her white lenses darted over her eyes, accusing the absent Ames. What little skin could be seen from her outfit of black and white striped and lace and torn gauze was mottled with goosebumps. "Models like her always have something going on, don't they? Someone they bribed to get on the cover of the magazine, someone they took drugs from to walk the catwalk. Girls like these have secrets."

George finally spoke. "Eden," he started. Somehow, his voice was smooth, as it always was. His blue eyes were clear and chiding and sure. "I don't think we need to go that far, come on. My impression was that Ames was a sweet young woman with the ability to pursue her dreams."

Tamanna heard Ilays whisper, "And by 'ability' they mean a skinny waist and a good face." She snorted. "Ability."

Beside her, Armand's fists tightened.

Eden was still talking. Now she looked straight into George's eyes, those blue, empty eyes, convincing him, and subsequently, everyone else. "Didn't you always see Ames typing on her phone? The entire time? You talk to her, she types. Ask her a question, she types. She's always typing and smiling at her phone."

"Maybe she's dating, or heard good news," Theresia offered, speaking for the first time.

"Young people nowadays are always on their phones anyway," Walter agreed loudly. He looked over at Evangeline, who nodded to the only thing she heard. "It isn't uncommon, especially when she didn't have anything else to do, or anyone else to talk to."

"But she did have someone to talk to," Tamanna put in suddenly. Walter continued to look at Evangeline, and George didn't pay her much attention - she was the young one. Somehow, they had discovered she was the teenager of the group. But Theresia and Ilays and Eden turned to look at her. Deaf Evangeline was still nodding to herself.

"She had someone to talk to," Tamanna said again. "Armand."

The officer absently looked up at them. "She—what? Oh, yeah, we talked for a bit."

George let out a measured sigh. "I don't see your point." "She was hiding something," Eden said. "I know it."

Theresia spoke again. "I agree with her. I don't think it's a good thing, but I think we should go through the phone. I condone it." Eden sighed heavily. "*Thank* you."

"Not because I think she has secrets," Theresia continued hastily, "But because there might be something in there that'll at least tell us if she really did abandon us, or if she was lost, or even kidnapped. She could have left a message. A clue." She looked each one in the eye, and suddenly, she wasn't the frail young mother that had seen her dead dog's body. She was somebody different. "Now Tamanna, get in that password again."

Tamanna obeyed, her fingers flashing with each digit pressed, and soon she had the phone unlocked and handed again to Theresia. She peered over her shoulder as they all crowded around the blonde woman. Theresia opened the phone app, and looked through Ames's recent calls.

She realized only later, what a terrible thing they'd done.

ARMAND

Ames had received tens —*hundreds*— of calls from someone called Sheila. Armand counted them silently as Theresia squeaked, and scrolled down. One hundred and eighty-two calls in the past two weeks. Of those one hundred and eighty-two calls, Ames had answered six. The profile picture was small and waiting to be picked up, and yet Theresia didn't touch it. She exited the app. "What am I looking for? What messages, what clues am I looking for?"

"Messages, the app," Armand found himself directing. "There could be something she left for us there." he tried to get the image out of his head—hundreds and hundreds of calls from one woman. A stalker, a creep? Someone hateful? Someone hurtful?

"Oh god," Theresia whispered. "Would you look at that?"

Armand focused on the phone. Theresia had opened up Ames's contact with this Sheila person. Sheila had been doing what they called spamming, sending messages over and over and over again. But the messages—

How could you?

Why would you do something like this?

This isn't a joke.

It isn't funny.

Stop it right now. Stop it, please.

You don't know what this could do.

Delete it. Please.

Please don't. Please.

Please.

Please.

Please stop.

Please.

What sickened Armand more was the little, single-worded replies from Ames. A woman begging and pleading the beautiful model, to stop something, to delete something. The beautiful model responding with winky faces. Smiley faces. Air-kiss emojis. Smug 'no, thank you's. Armand could see Ames typing again, her head bent down to the phone in her lap, scrolling for the perfect reply to desperate begging. Her lips smiling. The screen twinkling, tiny white rectangles reflecting in her eyes.

"This is what she was doing, smiling and texting?" Walter whispered. His voice rumbled through the silence like thunder rolling across the sky. "Keep scrolling."

Theresia reached the bottom of the chat, the most recent text. Ames's first long reply:

I've deleted them. I'm so sorry.

And all at once, all Armand could see was the misery in the woman's eyes, as her fingers trembled across the smooth surface of his little emoji pin -one of the emojis she had used in the chat, over and over again- and her soft words: *I would never, never run away.*

Armand felt betrayed. This stranger had betrayed his impression of her.

"What pictures?" Eden asked. Her hoarse voice, the voice that matched the appearance of its owner, broke the silence, the slow dawn of their collective realization. It felt as though everyone had to be snapped out of this new reality to respond to her.

"They're talking about some pictures," Eden continued. "What pictures?"

Theresia went to Ames's gallery, whispering, "She was blackmailing someone, wasn't she? She was a blackmailer. In the model industry. Models have secrets."

But Ames's gallery was empty. It was fully empty. It was chillingly empty.

There was not a single picture, not just of something horrendous, something terrible a woman called Sheila was caught doing, but of even Ames or anything else. No photoshoot pictures, no selfies, no daily makeup looks, no screenshots, nothing. It was fully empty. Theresia checked the trash, and it was empty too.

"So, she was blackmailing someone, doing something, and she was smiling about it," Ilays summed up. Armand turned to look at her. The woman's eyes were drawn tightly together, her mouth set in a firm line.

"Don't," Theresia said. She was right behind Armand. She was so far away. "Ilays, don't."

"I can't do anything anyway," Ilays snapped. "We're stuck here anyway, and no one knows when that goddamned driver is gonna come back—"

"But I know, and we all know what you're thinking," Theresia interrupted forcefully. "You're a reporter. It's natural to need to spread information to the public. But we don't even know what happened, really, to judge whose fault it was. And we don't know who Sheila is, or even where Ames is right now. So, whatever you're thinking, don't."

Ilays clenched her jaw, and glared at Theresia. Theresia stared right back.

Finally, Ilays turned away, and scoffed, "Reporter. I'm a *journalist.*"

The heaviness that lingered in the air, like a burden upon their shoulders, created something that felt, to Armand, as though the promise they'd made to stick with each other had been broken. If Ames —lovely, sweet Ames— was a blackmailer, another ruined piece of the modeling industry, what secrets could the others hold? Others that were not in the least hidden away by the flashing cameras, expensive clothing, and digital retouching that Ames had been, but were made of raw dirt, unhidden bloodshed, and proudly twisted thoughts?

Silently, they dispersed once again, some sitting back in the bus, some pacing around, but this time it felt as though they were walking away forever, abandoning them as Ames seemed to have. The model's phone was passed around for a moment, lingering in George's hands, before going to Walter, back to Theresia, to Eden, and disgustedly thrown to Ilays, before Armand found it placed in his hands. Ames's polished picture shown on the screen, smudged by fingerprints. The background was red, her dress exotic with clashing animal prints, varieties of fabrics, and agonizingly bright colors. She crouched, facing a side, her head turned to the camera alluringly. Her face was covered by the time display: 9:39 am.

Armand's fingers moved of their own volition. He typed in the password, unlocked the phone, and moved to the contacts app again, as Theresia had done before. He clicked on Sheila's contact information, on her profile picture.

From far away, when they scrolled past it before, it had looked like a blurry, innocent picture at a nightclub, or some such location. Not related to the history of Ames and Sheila, the emotional abuse that had passed between them. Ames had blackmailed this woman, taken pictures of her. Told her to do something, get her a part in a show or an event. Sheila had followed her order, gotten her the part, and Ames had toyed with her. Then Ames had suddenly changed her mind and deleted every single picture she'd taken, including the blackmail ones. She'd deleted all the pictures permanently. But she'd forgotten one.

The blackmail pictures. It was Sheila's profile picture; the one Ames had set for her. A woman hunched over a sink, staring at herself in the mirror. A credit card in her hand, as if she was paying someone. A smudge of white on the table before her. A powdered nose, with makeup and white dust.

Armand found himself staring at the picture for several seconds, then removing the profile picture, deleting it forever. He shut the phone off, pocketed it, and walked back to the bus. On the way, Walter stopped him. Large, white- skinned, muscled, dark-eyed, stubbled, intimidating, more like a bodybuilder than a gym coach. His archery duffel bag was slung across his shoulder. It was impossible to assume that the coach's spare clothes fit Armand the way they fit the coach himself.

"That's a damn shame," he said, and Armand didn't know if it was to himself or to someone else. "She was pretty, too."

Armand nodded lamely.

The coach continued, "It's kinda funny how no one thought of calling the police with her phone, huh? We were all scrambling for it a while ago."

Armand nodded again.

"Damn shame, though," Walter said again, and walked away.

Armand started on the bus. His first foot on the first metal step, his second foot hovering over the ground, he stopped.

Theresia had been standing behind the bus. She'd noticed the rabbit was gone. She stopped, looked one way, then the other way. She didn't notice Armand. Theresia silently slipped into the woods.

ONE YEAR AGO

A mes Perrault was a French girl. She didn't like the American stereotype of French people, with their berets, their exotic fashion and moustaches, their baguettes and perfumes, and their wines. But she'd been drinking the finest since she was sixteen, and she was a model, and so she had to admit that in the stereotype, she found some truth.

Ames loved her wine. She hated beer, and she hated rum, but she loved wine. So, it was no surprise when she decided to celebrate her twenty-first birthday at a cheese tasting event in America - the land of landless, the land of cultures, without a culture of its own. Ames invited her friends from her industry, and some of the high-profile celebrities she knew.

At one point of the party, she sat in a velvet booth with a charcuterie board before her, a glass of Syrah between her fingers, surrounded by her somewhat closer friends. There was a gorgeous black woman to her right, with a shaved head, diamond earrings and the gap-toothed smile that had won her a spot on a magazine cover three weeks ago. To her left was an older woman, somehow possessing more youth than the younger. She was built upon an invisible array of accolades that hung behind her wherever she went—the legacy she'd leave behind if ever she died. Whenever she died. And somehow this legacy had been built upon beauty, self-worth, self-righteousness, and talent. And somehow, she was Ames's friend.

"Darling, happiest of birthdays to you." The woman rolled her eyes a little.

"But this doesn't feel like a party."

It wasn't a party. It was a night of booze to forget the rejections she'd faced, the deadlines she didn't meet, and the qualifications she didn't pass disguised as a birthday party.

"I thought you'd enjoy it, Sheila." Ames looked straight into the model's dark brown eyes, lined with just the faintest crow's feet. "You don't like parties."

"I don't, but you do." Sheila took another few sips before putting her rosé down and standing up. "Let me use the restroom, and fix myself up while the party's still getting started."

She fluttered her eyes once more before walking off, adjusting her skirt.

Ames watched her go. She couldn't feel the smile on her lips. She turned away — and she nearly forgot about Sheila, until an hour had passed, and the model still hadn't returned. Ames wondered aloud, where she was.

The woman beside her leaned close to Ames and muttered, "She probably went home, secretly."

"She wouldn't do that to me." "She'd do that to anyone."

Ames felt a spike of irritation. "She doesn't have the nerve. She wouldn't leave. Not *my* party."

"She would —"

"My birthday party, no less. Twenty-first birthday party." Ames stood. "I'm not letting her leave. Where did she say she was?"

"The restroom."

Ames marched to the ladies' restroom. The door swung open. The floors and walls were marble, painted yellow by the lights twinkling from the wall lamps. Rows of quiet, half-empty stalls. A single person occupied the cold room - Sheila.

She was hunched over a sink. Third, to the left. Her heels squeaked on the marble every time she shifted.

"Sheila?"

The older woman looked up. Dazzling dark brown eyes. Dark brown eyelids. Tanned skin. A face of makeup. Red lips. White traces on her nose. Next to the sink was a barcode of white and marble. Her credit card trembled between her fingers.

This was when the life of Ames Perrault flashed before her eyes. Decisions, decisions, consequences, consequences. Every failure she'd experienced, ever success Sheila had. Every possibility, every risk, every path her life could go down, flashed before her eyes. In a span of a second, Ames saw the past and her entire future.

Then she focused on the present. Ames lifted her phone.

"Say cheese, darling."

THERESIA

The rabbit hadn't been hit by the bus. And now the rabbit was gone.

Theresia was surprised by the amount of time she'd spent staring at the dirt behind the still bus, the spot of dirt stained red. No one else seemed to notice, or care. Theresia did. She remembered the lifeless body of the rabbit, the lifeless body of Barnacles, the lifeless body of children crowded in a little room with walls of deep cracks and peeling paint. There had been so much blood. There would be so much more.

Theresia Pape found herself staring at the bloodied dirt behind the bus once again, feeling the morning breeze slip into her shirt. Dead bodies didn't just disappear, without a trace. Someone could have moved it, naturally. Theresia remembered the tears she had shed in front of those ladies, in front of the man who was apparently a police officer. One of them could have moved it to lessen her trauma. Theresia smiled.

Eden appeared to be walking back and forth, as she had been before. She saw Theresia, stopped, and smiled a little. Theresia returned to the smile.

"Don't mind me, I need to…" Eden gestured to the forest. "Be right back."

Theresia nodded and watched her go. The young lady was attired in black and white. She was probably not married. She probably did not have children.

Young, innocent, delicate children. Theresia remembered what she had said earlier: *I need to get there before he eats them.*

So, you can eat them first? Eden had replied. *They're delicious.*

Eden's back was disappearing into the trees. The girl marched with purpose. She wore a striped sweater, a long, lacy skirt, leg warmers, and a white shawl. The only color in her outfit was the hem of her shawl. It was red.

Theresia looked down at the bloodstain in the dirt. She looked back at the bus. No one was looking at her.

Theresia followed the girl silently. She slipped into the forest. The grass did not crunch under her, nor did the twigs snap. Even the wind held its breath as Theresia glided silently —as she did before, as she always did— through the trees.

Eden stopped. Theresia froze, and ducked behind a tree. She peered out, holding her necklaces in her fist so they would not clink together. Eden crouched, and pulled out a dark, murky green cloth from the floor of the woods. Something skin colored appeared. Long sticks of limbs, a glimpse of red hair.

Ames. The model.

Eden moved around Ames's body, and Theresia was finally given a clear glimpse. The girl was topless. The flesh of her side had been torn through, exposing white bone and what looked like the pale, smooth surface of an organ. Theresia pressed herself to the tree and watched. Eden sat cross legged before the corpse, and pulled out a knife. She tore off a chunk of Ames's flesh, and Theresia realized the gaping wound in the model's side was a result of the repeated action. She watched closely, carefully.

Eden held the flesh to her nose, then carefully ate it.

She ate meticulously, so that no blood or tendrils of flesh touched her makeup. She would tear, smell, eat, tear, smell, and eat. She ate her way through another sizeable chunk of Ames's flesh, occasionally stopping to throw away bits and pieces after sniffing at them. Eden ate quickly, then sorted through something by her side, something that was hidden by the eaten corpse. She pulled out a water bottle, spilled some water out, and cleaned her fingers. She dabbed her lips, tucked the water and her silver knife away, then stood.

Then she froze.

Theresia ducked back behind the tree, wondering for a second if she had been seen. When she heard no footsteps, no voices, nothing coming her way and accusing her, Theresia dared to peek out again.

Eden was staring straight ahead. Her eyes were wide, her white lenses still, fixed ahead. Her lips trembled. In her hand was the red-stained tip of her shawl, still draped and looped about her shoulders. She knew.

Theresia bit her lip. She pressed herself against the tree further, no longer spying on Eden. Ames's corpse —the eaten, twisted thing— entered her mind. She wouldn't be the next corpse. She wouldn't.

Eden's voice called out. "Is there someone there?"

Theresia clutched her necklaces and inhaled. Her shoe snapped a twig.

Eden's voice turned playful. "Who is it?"

Theresia refused to become like Ames's corpse. She refused it.

"You probably already saw me, didn't you?" There was a sharp sound, like a blade scratching against a fingernail, and

Theresia imagined the silver blade between Eden's pale, manicured fingers.

I'm not going to die, Theresia told herself. *I will not be eaten.*

Eden called out, "Would you like a bite?"

She will not eat me. I will not be eaten.

Theresia took a deep breath. Then she stood, and walked out to face Eden.

Eden's face was filled with fickle, momentary surprise. The white lenses glowed. Her black painted lips parted, then twitched in a smile of realization.

"Well, what do we have here?" She murmured. Theresia stood still. Eden advanced, closer and closer, like a predator hunting her long-awaiting prey. "The girl with trauma. The young, sweet mother. The lovely, innocent, gentle, beautiful young woman."

Theresia stared at Eden, straight at those lifeless, ghoulish white lenses. "I know what you did."

Eden turned back to the uncovered corpse. "Duh." "No, I know what you did."

Eden turned back to her. "And what was that I did?" "The rabbit's gone," Theresia said.

Eden's lips formed a brilliant, maniac smile. "Is that what you know I did?" she gestured to the body behind her. "Ames knew what I did, too."

"You ate the rabbit. The rabbit that was crushed, on the dusty road." "It wasn't that good."

Theresia gestured to Ames's gnawed corpse. "I suppose that was better?"

Eden nodded silently. Theresia smiled. She reached over and took the stained hem of the shawl from Eden's hand. "I can tell you went through a lot to get it."

Eden scowled.

Theresia continued, "I guess you'd want to kill me now, restock. But you

can't, can you?" She didn't let Eden answer. "Because then you'd have two bodies on your hand, and twice the risk of someone seeing them. You couldn't possibly eat through both me *and* Ames before someone, someone like me, finds you. Then you'll have to kill them too. How troublesome. But you can't let me go, either.

Because then," Theresia leaned closer, "I'd run off and talk."

Eden's pale face looked gray. The cannibal, the sly, inhuman predator had been backed into a corner. "What are you saying?"

"I'm not saying anything," Theresia said. "I'm only suggesting that we make a deal."

"What deal?"

"You swear not to kill me, you stick by my side, and I feed you. After all, it was me who put the rabbit there."

TWENTY YEARS AGO

Twenty years really isn't too long ago, but if one found themselves in a world twenty years ago, certainly they'd be surprised. Theresia Pape was seven years old. Even at seven, Theresia had a little stroller in her arms, with her dolly sleeping in it. The doll was scribbled on with her mother's lipstick and her markers, and the yarn hair was tangled with Theresia's plastic hair ties.

Even at seven, Theresia wanted to be a mother. She went nowhere without her favorite doll, Theresa — she'd named it so because she'd always liked it if her name had been spelled without the *i* — and her favorite thing to do was push Theresa in her stroller, round the garden. Theresia and Theresa were inseparable, people would say teasingly. But of late, Theresa had been staying away from Theresia, hiding in the back of the closet, never sitting in her stroller. Theresia hadn't been playing with her favorite doll.

The truth was, Theresia was afraid. She'd been feeling angry — so, incredibly, unnecessarily angry — for arbitrary reasons. Her mother wore a blue floral dress — it made Theresia angry. She thought it made her mother look like the curtains. Her elder sister came home from high school at two in the afternoon instead of two-ten — it made her angry. She was now lacking ten extra minutes of time alone. The dog would bark and bark and bark — and it made her angry. The dog wouldn't have to grow up and go to school and have a job. What was it so angry about?

Two weeks ago, in this anger, Theresia had quietly snuck to the refrigerator in the middle of the night, and pulled out the fresh peas her mother had soaked in water a while ago. She took up a fistful and squished them until the green, sad paste leaked from the cracks between her fingers and ran down from the sides of her clenched fist, down her arm. It had felt so good. Then, a week ago, when her mother made jelly, she'd taken her portion to her room, and mashed it between her fingers again. It wasn't enough. She wanted to rip the jelly apart and watch the condensation leak off and spray onto the table at which she sat and, on the wall, and sprinkle on her face.

It made her so, so afraid. The little girl wanted to rip something apart. She wanted to hurt. She wanted to hurt everything, but she didn't want to hurt her doll. She didn't know how to protect her from her feelings. She didn't know who else to hurt but the poor stuffed girl that sat in her closet, the fluff ripped out and the hair torn out and the face scribbled on.

Theresia knew there was something wrong with her only when she caught herself red-handed, peeling off the stitches of the patches that made for Theresa's eyes. She saw the ruined doll in her hands, silently, desperately destroyed without the world knowing, and knew she was special. She tried to stop herself that night. Theresia gently placed Theresa in a box under her bed, and cried herself to sleep that night. She kept her hands to herself, tucking them tightly to her chest even as they shook, trembled, and itched to shoot out. She trimmed the fingernails she had grown out to scratch at the paint on the walls, pretending it was skin. She controlled herself, like a zookeeper controlling a rabid animal, and went to sleep.

It didn't last. Theresia woke up in the middle of the night with an unquenchable thirst, and she knew what she needed to do. She knew the one thing she could not live without. It hurt her, but it made her happy more.

Right then, in the middle of the night twenty years ago, Theresia tiptoed out of bed. She tried to cry, and feel guilty for what she wanted to do, what she dreamed of doing, but she couldn't. She couldn't feel guilty for hurting, and that made her feel guilty.

In truth, Theresia had no idea what she was doing. She walked around a bit, drank a glass of water in hopes that this metaphorical thirst could be literally quenched. She left the house and walked about the garden in her pajamas, hoping the night air would soothe her urges.

That was when she saw it - the dog. A white labrador retriever her mother had rescued off a road as a puppy. It had grown up with her, now three years old. Buffy Barnacles, four-year-old Theresia had named it. Barnacles. Barnacles hated tomatoes but loved tomato juice. He whimpered and pretended to limp when they took him to the park so he wouldn't have to interact with the other dogs. He barked happily at passing cars.

He barked so, so much.

Barnacles saw her as she walked around the garden. He wagged his tail but did not bark. He knew people slept when the sky was dark, and he liked to keep quiet. He tromped up to her and asked for pets with his little seal eyes and his happy face. His mouth hung open dumbly, innocently, tongue lolling out, panting. His feet hopped up and down, taking little steps, doing his little dance for pets like a street performer dancing for money.

Theresia didn't see it happening either. She saw his pale fur against the night sky, looked into his eyes - and the next moment, his eyes were open and dead, and he lay on the ground instead of on his feet. The bloodied metal end of their garden hose dripped from her hands. She stared at the scene with surprise. Then she dropped the hose, and turned it on. Water trickled from the pipe. She washed off the blood, turned the hose off, then lifted Barnacles.

In her arms, it seemed as though the puppy only slept. In her arms, he was still alive.

Theresia carried Barnacles to the fence, where her house ended and the neighbors began. She dumped the body over the other side of the fence, then hopped over herself. She slipped on the gardening gloves that she knew the balding Mr Harrison worked with on weekends, took in her hands his little metal shovel, looked around into the empty dead night, then bludgeoned her puppy, wishing she hadn't done the same to Theresa.

When Theresia woke up the next morning to her mother and father's horrific screaming, the neighbors' shouts and cries, she couldn't bring herself to smile or remember. She listened to the words being hurled around with emotion, to the looming police sirens that followed, the footsteps and the yelling and the crying and the events unfolding slowly like a prewritten destiny, and she thought to herself that it would have felt better if she'd used her own hands instead of a shovel.

Next time, she decided, and went back to sleep.

TAMANNA

Tamanna had watched a lot of detective movies, a lot of murder mysteries.

Being a teenager in the twenty-first century made one not very ignorant about terrible things that happen to people. But it was the first time she'd been stuck in one of those situations. Wasn't it only in movies that a person got stuck in the middle of nowhere with someone that went missing, then turned out to be a blackmailer?

Curiosity chewed at her. Her cat was being killed. She desperately wanted to know what Ames had blackmailed the other woman with. She'd never find out, and that was the worst part. Curiosity, the poison that killed all the characters in those murder mysteries, filled her wholly, made her itch and her palms sweat and her skin shiver. She couldn't stop thinking about it.

Tamanna decided finally that she needed to get it out of her head. She needed a distraction. She contemplated going up to Armand and saying, 'heck of a party bus, huh?' but he looked utterly shaken. *Did he like Ames? He talked to her a lot in the start.* She decided to leave him alone. She looked around, and found Evangeline sitting there calmly in the bus, fiddling with her blocky cellphone.

Armand's words played through her head. A book about organs. Memory loss. She shuffled from her seat to that of the old lady's, and said, "Hi, Evangeline! How are you?"

The woman looked up. She had cataract, and her sallow skin was dotted with what could have been freckles, or a skin infection. "Hi, dear. You'd look nicer without your glasses."

Tamanna sighed, and sat next to her.

"There's something happening outside," Evangeline said, not looking up from her phone. "They won't tell me what happened. I suppose they haven't told you, either. You're a young girl, after all."

Tamanna didn't really feel like explaining the situation to Evangeline, and so she didn't. Instead, she pointed clearly to the phone the old lady was fiddling with and asked, "Do you need any help with that?"

Evangeline looked up and scowled in impatience. "Of course, I do! It's so difficult, it's all so difficult now. Everyone uses these phones and these gadgets. No one can write a proper letter anymore."

"I agree," Tamanna said, not agreeing.

"No one!" Evangeline said again. "No one can write a proper letter nowadays. Back when I was your age, we all had better eyesight and better handwriting."

And less trees. "So, you need help with that? Sending an email, or texting-"

"We all peacefully sat near our fireplaces and desks and thought out meaningful things and wrote them down and sent them. No thoughtless texts that you can just delete. So many meaningless things so say, nothing important nowadays." she gestured with her head to the windows. "Look at them all, saying so many things at once. I bet they don't mean half the things they say."

She pulled out a folded piece of paper from her bag and waved it under Tamanna's nose. "We used to write like this all the time, see?"

She unfolded it, and showed it off. An old piece of paper, torn at the edges, with neat cursive writing inside. "See, that's the address right there—the address and the recipient go on the envelope—that's who we're writing to, and look at that. Look at all that. My friend wrote this to me thirty years ago. He meant every word. Look at all that, look at how much he wrote. He meant all of it."

Tamanna stared at it in fascination. History—though thirty years ago certainly, isn't history—was something so beautiful to her. She'd always loved history. When she learnt about it in school, something would gnaw at her. It wasn't just a passion or a fascination. It was something that actually touched her soul, like a single petal falling across a still pond, creating momentary ripples but the memory of a lifetime. It was heartbreaking, and it was painful, her hiraeth for the past. Was it even possible, to miss something you never experienced, to dearly want to go back to past days you were never part of?

"May I?" she asked tenderly, and reached out for the paper. How she wished to be a part of history, even the recent history. She knew the past was as flawed as the future, that the past wasn't a perfect world. But to the people that lived in it, it was once the present, and that was so incredibly incredible.

Evangeline muttered something, but she nodded and absently handed the letter over. "As long as you help me with this later. You're a dear girl. I see you writing in that little book all the time. The only girl I've seen of your age writing, instead of staring at a little screen all day. I like you, yes I do."

Tamanna nearly didn't even thank her. She took the paper with fingers that trembled to uncover those hidden folds of the fabric of the past.

"Dear? Dear, move aside. I'll go ask that nice handsome fellow in the suit if there's something else to eat." Evangeline nearly pushed Tamanna out of the seat with those bony hands of hers. Tamanna moved out of the way, and back to the posterior of the bus, where she was sitting before, and unfolded the letter.

It was from a Nathan Colbert. Colbert's handwriting was a slanted, straight cursive, where every lowercase letter seemed to be the same size, with no dips and uneven markings. Tamanna slowly read.

Miss B. Joanna-Marie,

Words cannot describe what power you hold in your fingertips. Mightier is the hand that holds the pen than that which holds the sword, is what they say, but I think mightier is your hand, which holds both at the appropriate time in which they should be held. I saw your work myself. I was a mere intern at the time of the famous Myer performance. I was spellbound by your clean movements and the efficiency with which you performed. And a performance it was, truly. The movements of your hand, though bloodier, were no less than the movements of a director of orchestra! And Myer was your symphony.

I hope to achieve your level of agility someday. And I hope you will guide me someday. I plan to take part in your business. My interviews begin the next week, and I am told in full faith that I will pass them. This new step in career excites me, though not as much as the prospect of someday working alongside your person. I hope you receive me with open arms. To the best future of futures, and to the riches that might soon follow.

Your admirer, Nathan Colbert.

Tamanna read the letter. The writing, the style, everything - it was so old-fashioned, so perfect. But that wasn't what she saw. *My friend wrote this to me, thirty years ago. My friend wrote this to me.*

To me.

The letter was addressed to B. Joanna-Marie.

Tamanna looked up and around. *And so, the case begins.* Armand stood outside, arms crossed, looking out impatiently, nervously, as though he still had hope that the driver would return. Tamanna stumbled off the bus and ran to him.

"Armand. Armand! You won't believe! Remember what you said, all that mystery around Evangeline? You won't believe what-" "Not now," he muttered.

"Huh?"

"Not now. Please. Not you too." "What are you talking about?"

"I don't want you getting into danger. Get back on the bus." he finally turned to look at her, barely moving his lips as he spoke, eyes twitching around. "Get back on the bus, please. Tell me later, okay?"

Tamanna didn't know what it was. It sounded stupid to call it a gut instinct.

But from the way Armand, the good-natured samaritan, looked around so nervously, acted so weirdly, she knew she shouldn't bother him. Was he still ruminating about Ames? Was it someone else now? Whatever it was, Tamanna walked away, leaving him alone.

She bumped into the journalist on the way back to the bus. The woman was tall, dark skinned, her hair unseen behind a blue hijab with pretty embroidering.

Ilays was her name, if Tamanna remembered correctly. She remembered Armand saying he had talked to Ilays about the book Evangeline had given her.

Tamanna tugged on the girl's sleeve. Ilays looked down. "Can I help you?" "Ilays, right?"

"Yes."

"You're the one that Evangeline lent her book to? *Know Your True Value*, or something?"

Ilays frowned. *"Know Your True Worth, yes."*

Tamanna smiled, and lowered her voice. "Armand told me that you told him-" she gestured to where he stood, in case Ilays did not remember. "He told me that you told him the book was actually about organs, and their value or something?"

"Yeah, it was."

"And also, that Evangeline has dementia, so she can't remember anything about the book? What did she say?"

Ilays thought for a second. "Well, I told her that I never expected her to read a book about organs, and she told me she didn't know why she had it either, just that she did. She's had it with her for a long time. She told me about the dementia home after, when I pressed."

"She's always had it with her, huh? You think she's had it with her for, say, thirty years at least?"

Ilays nodded. "The book itself was published in the seventies, eighties. I checked."

Tamanna smiled triumphantly. She reminded herself to take note of the entire thing in her journal. "Well, I might have found something. If you're in for it."

Ilays grinned. She had a silver crown in the left side of her jaw. "I'm a journalist. Of course, I'm in."

Tamanna leaned in closer. "So, Evangeline seemed to be having trouble with her phone, so I asked her if she needed help. She started saying these stuffs, you know, typical old people stuff, about how people don't write letters anymore. Then she showed me this letter she had from thirty years ago, kind of showed me the way it was written. She said it was written by a friend, *to her*. Now look at this."

Tamanna showed her the letter, and once it was fully read, tapped on the recipient's name. "B. Joanna-Marie. She said it was to *her*. Evangeline. She said it so surely… What?"

Ilays had gone wide-eyed. She squinted at the paper again. "That doesn't make…"

"What? What is it?" Tamanna hissed.

Ilays scoffed with undisguised shock. She walked away. Tamanna started to follow her, but stopped abruptly when the journalist tapped on Evangeline's shoulder. They talked for a moment. George, the man in the suit, watched them. He caught Tamanna's eye. Evangeline pulled out the very book —*Know Your*

True Worth – from her large purse with a smile, said something, and handed it to Ilays.

Ilays returned triumphantly. "What is it?" Tamanna attempted again.

Ilays held the book up. Her finger tapped the bottom.

Know Your True Worth. An encyclopaedia on inner values. Published in 1978. Authored by Joanna-Marie Blocker.

Tamanna looked up in awe. "Does that mean-"

Ilays grinned. "If we're stuck here anyway, why not…"

Tamanna held out a hand. It quivered before her. Ilays shook it.

"I'm Tamanna," Tamanna said. "And it's so, so good to meet you."

ARMAND

It was her seventh time in half an hour. Seventh time in half an hour that Eden had snuck off into the woods, saying she needed pee.

The scarf she had worn, the one Armand had seen most certainly painted red, as if the fabric itself was bleeding and injured, had appeared after Ames had gone missing, and had suddenly disappeared, one trip to the forest later.

It had awakened something in Armand. He was an officer. He wasn't a particularly good one, but he had some experience in knowing when something wasn't right. Armand found himself leaning against the side of the bus, staring at the particular crook of the bush that bent every time Eden walked through into the forest. *Maybe she's pregnant.*

"Hey there."

Armand turned. Walter stood behind him, arms crossed, peering out at the spot Armand had been moments ago. "Something on your mind? Something other than… all this, you know."

Armand shook his head numbly. "Man, it's just been wild, huh?" He moved back slowly —slowly, prey-like, to prove to Walter he wasn't dangerous— until his back hit the side of the pink bus.

"It has been," Walter agreed. "I've been trying to get it all out of my head, but I just don't know how. I guess talking helps."

Armand recognized the invitation. Still resting against the bus, he turned to face his company. Walter watched him. Something shifted in those dark eyes.

Armand couldn't tell what it was. Walter cleared his throat, and asked, "How old are you?"

"Excuse me?"

"How old are you, man?"

It wasn't *if you don't mind me asking, how old are you?* Or *if you're comfortable answering, how old are you?* It was an interrogation, not an inquisition.

Armand cleared his throat, suddenly uncomfortable. "Twenty-three. Why?" Walter shook his head. "I heard that girl say you were a cop?"

"Yeah. I'm a detective at the police department." "And you're twenty-three?"

"Yeah. I just got promoted, though, so…" "How'd you do it so young?"

Armand squirmed. He didn't know the answer. It was like he couldn't remember it. He forced the discomfort away and answered, "I got lucky with a drug bust. I'd been a uniformed officer for a year or so, doing speed traps on the highway. Then I uncovered a drug ring and took it down, and I got a promotion."

Walter looked at him approvingly. Then he, too, joined Armand in leaning against the side of the bus. They stood there for several quiet minutes, as if they really were friends, as if they'd known each other for so much longer than an hour and a half, as if they weren't only talking with each other to forget their miserable plight.

It was then that Armand truly realized how tall the archery coach was. The man was easily six and a half feet tall, and perhaps half as thick around the shoulders, and hunched back of a man that had gotten used to every room being far too suffocating, every doorway being too little. And he was close. So, so close to Armand that it felt — despite the fact that they stood out in broad daylight, amid the morning breeze — as though just the two of them were cramped in a little utility closet, with nowhere to go. Armand stood there for a moment, assessing this feeling of newfound claustrophobia, and when that moment had passed, Walter shifted, and it was impossible to think he hadn't come even closer.

Then came the rough hand on his shoulder. It did not rest on his left shoulder, the one closer to Walter in the manner they stood, but snaked around the back of Armand's neck and placed itself on the ball of his right shoulder. Armand immediately straightened, senses flaring, and started to move away, but the hand dug into him, fingers stabbing into his skin and bones, and kept him there.

Walter bent and murmured, "Don't try a thing. Detective or not."

Armand closed his eyes. He imagined himself in his uniform, from before the promotion, instead of the coach's ill-fitting tracksuit, wearing his badge, holding his gun, aiming fire at something deadly and terrifying. "What are you doing?" he muttered.

"I said keep it cool, kid. Do as I say. I'm going to go to George and tell him to give the others more food that I have - that'll keep them occupied. You stay right here. Don't move."

Armand opened his eyes and looked around, acting casual. "And what if I don't?"

It was a surprisingly unintelligent thing to say. Even if that long bag Walter carried with him was devoid of the weapon he was skilled at wielding, the man could easily kill Armand. All it took was a secluded place and his two hands. And unfortunately, Walter seemed well aware of it. At the question, he raised his eyebrows as if he was asking *did you really just ask me that?* And with no further response, patted Armand's cheek -almost gently- and walked away.

Armand looked out at the road. It stretched on before disappearing behind a curve of trees on one end. On the other, it faded into the distance of the forest. Not a soul was in sight besides the party bus and its people. Armand wondered how quickly he could run. Heart racing, crossing his arms close to his chest, not knowing what he planned to do, Armand walked out into the middle of the road.

He saw Walter's head turn his way. He ignored it. He had nowhere to go anyway. Despite the looming threat above him, he didn't feel scared.

Then he saw Tamanna running towards him. Her eyes were wild, her mouth slack open and grinning, and she clutched a piece of paper in her left hand.

"Armand."

Panic hit him.

"Armand!"

It doused him in fear and overwhelmed him, taking over his sight and pushing into his ears and nostrils and drying up his eyeballs. He imagined Walter running up to them —so vividly that it felt, for a second, that Walter really was running to them— and grabbing Tamanna and squeezing her neck and killing her instantly, before turning to Armand with fury. *I told you not to move!*

"You won't believe! Remember what you said, all that mystery around Evangeline? You won't believe what-"

"Not now," Armand said. He found himself muttering it, barely moving his lips, and he found himself staring at Walter, waiting for the man to find out.

"Huh?"

"Not now."

Walter turned, stared at the back of Tamanna's head, then looked into Armand's eyes. "Please."

Armand didn't know what he said afterwards. He stared straight at Walter, murmuring and muttering and utterly terrified until Tamanna —the poor, innocent girl— shrugged and walked-jogged away. She stopped and started talking to Ilays. When her attention was no longer on Armand, Walter lifted a hand and beckoned for Armand to approach.

Armand started walking. He felt tense from the anticipation of what was to come, but the moment Tamanna had left —the moment anyone else but him had escaped the imminent danger of Walter's wrath— the fear had left with her. His heart raced, but he wasn't scared.

Walter beckoned again, and Armand joined him. Standing with them were George and Evangeline. The short old woman licked her lips, fumbling to open a packet of Doritos. George had Walter's archery bag over his shoulder. He asked, "Want one?"

It took Armand a moment to realize the question was directed to him. He shook his head. George smiled reassuringly, pulled out a giant fistful of more snacks, and returned the thin bag to Walter, who slung it over his shoulder. "Don't stray too far away, guys. We don't want a repeat with what happened to that poor model. And if you find the road close by, don't run away without us. It isn't right."

Armand had no clue what the man was talking about. He watched George walk away with the snacks. He handed Ilays and Tamanna some, then moved into the bus, where Eden, Theresia, and Evangeline were. He nearly forgot about it, forgot about everything that had happened in the last five minutes, until Walter's hand —that awful, heavy hand— clamped around his shoulder again. "Come on."

It wasn't a request. It wasn't even an order. Walter walked away from the bus, and Armand walked with him.

"Where are we going?" He hated how childish he sounded. "Shs. Walk."

Armand crossed his arms, feeling thin and weak inside the oversized tracksuit, and continued walking silently. He walked this way until Walter's hand left his shoulder. Before he could comprehend his freedom, the hand grabbed his arm, he was yanked, the forest suddenly surrounded them, and the world became slightly darker. Armand found himself somewhere between the greenery, the road just escaping the peripheral of his vision. Walter had him pinned to a tree. The coach's thick forearm hovered over his neck —not choking him, yet crushing him in its grip, reminding him of what it could do— and forcing his chin up. Armand looked up, into Walter's eyes.

"The hell are you-" "Shhh."

It was almost soothing, gentle. Armand stopped talking and focused on his breathing. What a situation—what a terrible situation he'd gotten himself into. He waited patiently for Walter to say something. The man worked his jaw, and took his time in sizing Armand up before finally speaking.

"I told them we were going out to search for the driver. They know you're a cop, so they trust you, and I'm the guy with the food, so they trust me."

Armand stayed silent. Walter worked his jaw some more, as if he was thinking —but from Armand's point of view his brain seemed more on the empty side— and then spoke again.

"You know something, don't you?"

"Like what?" Armand said finally. He wasn't afraid, and he'd come to terms with that, but now he felt something akin to irritation, and that surprised him.

"I don't know," Walter replied, almost teasingly, and Armand felt the irritation grow. "I know you know something."

"Like *what*?" Armand snapped. The next moment he felt Walter's forearm press against his neck, and suddenly he couldn't breathe anymore.

"Hey. *Hey*. Look at me." Walter looked down at him, into his eyes, almost meaningfully. "You answer what I want you to answer. No attitude with me here, or I'll make your short, short life hell. Got it?"

Armand glared.

"Stop glaring. I said, *got it?*"

Armand glared harder. He realized, then, how desperately one needed air to survive, and so he gave up and nodded the best he could.

"Good. Now tell me what I need to know. You know something about someone on the bus, don't you? You suspect someone of something."

"I don't know what you're—"

"Cut the crap. I know that look you've been getting for a while now, since that model disappeared. You think one of them is involved? You think it was murder? You see something you shouldn't have seen? Whatever it is on your mind, I want to hear it now. *Now.*"

Armand decided it would be dangerous to ask why he cared so much.

Instead, he tapped Walter's forearm with his fingers and looked up meaningfully. The coach stared at him suspiciously for several seconds—as if he was worried that Armand would kidnap *him*—and finally removed his arm and stepped away. With the pressure lifted, Armand felt a new wave of pain seep into his back from being rubbed against the bark. He stumbled away from the tree and regained his breath. That short moment felt perhaps like the only moment in which he had some ounce of control in the entire situation, and it embarrassed him.

Armand straightened and looked Walter straight in the eye. He considered bolting, but it was sure to be a futile attempt, so instead he found himself answering Walter's demand.

"Eden," he said. "I think Eden had something to do with Ames's disappearance."

"Why?"

"She ran off to 'find' Ames and when she came back and Ames didn't, the hem of that white scarf -or whatever it is she's wearing- was stained red. It looked like blood. And then when we found Ames's phone, she was trying so hard to find *something* wrong, something on Ames's phone. It just felt like she knew there was something there and wouldn't let us give up. It made me wonder—" Armand stopped. Every ounce of his being screamed at him to shut up, to not reveal another thing, as if, by exposing his suspicions around Eden, he'd put himself or Tamanna in danger. Walter sensed the hesitation. He crossed his arms—a simple, clear gesture, to show that his arms, the very arms that choked Armand a second ago, still existed. Armand sighed, and continued. He had too much to lose. "I... I couldn't help but wonder if she already knew about Ames blackmailing that other model before we did, okay? That's why she seemed to hate Ames so much and that's why she insisted Ames abandoned us, to make us hate her too, and that's why she—well, that could be why she murdered Ames. If she did at all. I don't know. It's just the hint of a theory. Happy now?"

"Ecstatic," Walter muttered absently.

Armand rubbed his throat, venturing out on a limb. "Why do you care so much?"

Walter glared down at him.

"Why do you care about what I think at all, huh?" Armand pressed. "I mean, what about what I think was so important that you needed to..." *blow your cover?* Was that what it was? "That you needed to threaten me out here?"

Walter worked his jaw again —that infuriating, shifting jaw- and said quietly,

"Eden. So, you suspect Eden."

"No one else is suspicious," Armand snapped. "Why was it so important-" "Shut up!" Walter turned around. Then he stopped, turned back slowly, and looked at Armand. He shrugged. "You know what, it's not like you're going to do anything about it, now, huh? Why not? I care so much about what you think because you saw something, kid. You were the only one that saw anything, other than me. I saw something too."

"What did you see?"

Walter looked like he was contemplating telling Armand anything. But he did, eventually, and the thought that there was nothing that needed to hold his secrets back made Armand queasy.

"What did I see?" Something frail entered Walter's massive body. "That girl. The one with the stroller."

"Theresia?"

"That's her name? Theresia. Well, it was her. I didn't notice a thing off with the goth girl."

"What did you see Theresia do?"

"The rabbit," said Walter. "I was off walking around the back of the bus, looking for a trunk, when I saw the rabbit. It was alive when the bus was stopped. I saw it myself, hopping from the forest to the back of the bus. First, I ignored it."

Armand listened silently to the dramatic description. He didn't know Walter was the type to explain his memories like that.

Walter continued, "So I ignored it. I walked over to the back, but I stopped when I saw something moving—a coach's instincts, that's all. I moved forth a bit, found myself looking at that girl Theresia's back. I knew it was her, because she's the only one wearing that bright red shirt. I was going to go ask her if there was a trunk, but then, I heard bones breaking. It was that clear sound, the *crunch.*

Crunch. Crunch. That sound. And I thought she might be hurt, but I thought it was strange that she wasn't making a sound while she was getting her bones broken. The moment I remembered that rabbit that had hopped over to where she was, she moved, and I thought she might have seen me, so I ran back away from there. Then she started screaming and crying about how the bus ran over a rabbit."

Armand wondered, for a single second, if Walter, moments ago, had really choked him to death, and from all his past sins— heaven knew he had plenty of those—he had arrived in hell. "Theresia? The mother? You're saying you saw her…"

Walter nodded. "She killed that rabbit."

Armand shuddered. "Why would she do that?" "I don't know, man. That's just twisted."

"But the rabbit's gone now, isn't it? Where is it?"

"Is it gone?" Walter asked. "I didn't know that. I stopped going 'round the back entirely after that."

"Well, it's gone. Ames is gone. Eden keeps running off to the forest. And now Theresia's in it too—*god.*"

"This is messed up," Walter mumbled. Armand looked up at the man, ruminating. Walter was scared. He was only scared.

"So, what are you going to do?" Armand asked.

Walter was silent. Far too silent. He fiddled with the straps of his bag, then shoved his left hand into his pocket. Then he looked up, straight into Armand's eyes with his own—that were not so blue but just as haunting as George's- and smiled. Just a little, just a twitch of a smile, but to Armand it could have been a gleeful cackle.

"You mean, what are *you* going to do?" Walter said. His voice was now suddenly quiet, and something about every inch of his frame was sinister. "You're going to spy on them, of course. If Eden's got something to do with it, and

Theresia's out crushing little critters, who knows who else is out to get us?"

"Hey, man, I've told you everything I know." Armand's legs pushed him backwards, of their own accord. "I don't want to get involved with them. For all we know, they could be the reason Ames is *dead*."

"Exactly," Walter said. "I'm not putting myself in their path. I'm not getting myself crushed like that rabbit, and I'm not going to go missing. But I want to keep myself safe, and to do that I need you."

"What," Armand snapped. "You want me to do your dirty work? I'm not doing *jack* – "

Walter moved far too quickly for someone of his size. The next thing he knew, Armand was back up against the tree, but this time there was no forearm against his neck. Instead, Walter had in his hand a handkerchief, dampened with something sweet and cloying and numbing. He pressed the cloth against Armand's mouth.

They could have stood like that for hours, days, weeks, or months. Years and years passed. All Armand could smell was sweetness, and all he could see was Walter's face—amused, curious, but not for a single moment evil. Psychopathic.

The sweet smell faded away with Armand's eyesight. His vision and the smell seemed to physically clasp hands, hum a tune, and skip away with each other like lovers on a beach. From there, Armand couldn't see anything, and he couldn't smell anything. He couldn't breathe or move or speak. Instead, he was filled with pain—numbing, searing pain that was so wholly indescribable that he couldn't find the part of his being needed to cry out, to make it stop. He didn't know what part of him hurt so terribly, whether it was a physical or a mental pain, whether it was terrible or awful, or when it would stop. It became his whole world. He felt the pain. He saw the pain. He reached out and touched the pain. He tasted the pain.

Armand found himself in a dark abyss, with nothingness in front of him and nothingness behind him, or above or underneath him. The only thing that existed in that world, besides himself, was the glowing white sphere of pain. It presented itself as a crystal with sharp shard and blinding reflections and no matter what he tried to do, or make himself do, he could not look away from it and he could not pull away from it. He was trapped and hurt and wounded and injured and—

THERESIA

A second round of snacks was distributed later on. The handsome man, George, had resorted to opening a can of protein powder and mixing it with the water bottles they had to create a substance to survive off. Theresia knew it wasn't even a last resort. They were desperate, starving, and hopeless.

And yet, of the eight people that remained milling around the pink bus, not a single person seemed to want to call the police or the tow truck services and go home. Every time Theresia thought of it, or saw the evidence of it around her, her heart would leap up and about, and she knew something was wrong.

As for herself, she didn't want to leave. Not now. She looked at Eden, who stood to a side, sipping a bottle of water. Did it taste like blood to her? Did Eden think of a corpse every time she ate? Eden caught Theresia's gaze, made a little biting gesture, and winked.

Theresia beamed.

She joined Eden on the road, and together, they stared off at the rest of the people on the bus.

"I've never done it to a human, you know," Theresia said quietly. "Why not?"

"More risk and repercussions. And they aren't so small. Only the kids are small enough."

Eden turned to her suspiciously. "The stroller...is that - is that why you had

kids?"

Theresia bit back a smile. "You think I killed my kids? That I had kids just to crush 'em?"

"What else could they be for?"

Theresia looked over and winked, feeling light and airy like the wind.

"That's a story for another day, sweetie."

Eden's lips —lips that had licked off blood less than an hour ago- soundlessly

whispered, "oh." She smiled a little. "So how do we get on to the next person?" "Slow down, cowgirl. You haven't finished the first."

"You could help out with that."

Theresia wrinkled her nose. "Ew, first of all. Second of all, I'd want you to have it. Enjoy. You probably don't get much around the city. Too many people."

"You guessed it." Eden grinned. "I like how you can see right through me.

Like an X-ray. You can see my thoughts and my hopes and my bones."

And break them, Theresia wanted to say. Instead, she shrugged and smiled, feeling hopelessly proud. Of course, whether or not the entire human-killing business went well enough, she'd have to kill Eden at the end anyway, or she'd turn up as a half-eaten corpse when it was all done, but thinking about it almost *hurt.* It was as if she actually liked Eden.

"So?" Eden's voice broke her thoughts. "Whenever I'm done with Ames, how do we get on to the next one?"

Theresia shrugged. "I thought you had a plan. How did you get on with Ames?"

Eden scowled. "She saw me eating the rabbit."

"Oof. That's low." Theresia hesitated. "Is that why we found her phone?" "What do you mean?"

"Her phone, on the side of the road. Was it you're doing?"

Eden smiled, and shrugged. "I found out about the blackmailing. Turns out our pretty model isn't as clean as she tastes. I thought it would be fun if you guys found out, too, so…" she shrugged again. "Never mind that. How do we get on to the next one?"

"Oh, you naughty, naughty you." Theresia grinned and shook her head. "I'm thinking I tell someone about that scarf you ridiculously carried around, the one I caught you with. Tell them about it. They get suspicious, we offer to follow you, and then *boom*."

Eden nodded. "You get free therapy, I get food. Sounds like a plan. I want them to know about the rabbit and Ames, though."

"*And* we're a braggadocio." Theresia shook her head. "Is there anything the goth girl isn't?"

"Shut up—" Eden stopped abruptly. "Hey, look. Walter's back." "Who?"

"The coach guy, the big muscular one. Look, he's back. He took the cop with him, but I don't see…"

Theresia saw him too. The coach that had given them his food -Walter- was back, walking from the twisted road before them. His bag, the one George had taken the food from, was over his shoulder, but the young cop he'd gone with wasn't there.

Theresia nearly laughed.

"Where do you think he is?" she whispered.

Eden shrugged. "I don't know. Unless Walter killed him."

Theresia felt a scowl form on her face. "We have company, huh?"

"What's up with him and the cop anyway?" Eden suddenly clasped Theresia's arm. She had a frown upon her heavily made face, one of genuine, deep curiosity. It was a strange expression on her usually sardonic face. "I mean, you saw them walking off, didn't you?"

"What do you mean?"

"I think they're doing something together. They're all chummy now. When we were all just hanging out, Walter had his arm around Armand —" "Armand?"

"The cop. Walter had his arm around him. He had his arm around Armand's shoulder when they were walking off to look for the driver again."

It was as if Walter knew they were talking about him. When Theresia and Eden began walking towards the group that was now assembling around Walter, the gym coach stared up suddenly — with eyes like two snipers, targeting and shooting bullets at them — and watched Theresia. He looked at Eden, then back at Theresia again.

"He's back there," Walter was saying as they got closer to the group that had formed. "My phone slipped out of my bag and got lost somewhere, and he's out searching for it. Told me to get back so none of you would get worried."

"So, you left him there?" asked the teenage girl. She pushed up her glasses angrily. Walter shook his head, almost sincerely.

"No, no. Like I said, he told me to come back here so you guys wouldn't get worried. I just came back to let you guys know we're all okay, but we can't seem to find the main roads. Its forest as far as we walk. There might be something further, but we can't walk all the distance."

Theresia scowled. She watched carefully, not too suspiciously, as Walter took a few water bottles and a couple of packets of chips for himself and the cop to continue their quests as the unofficial searchers of the missing driver. He stored them in his archery bag. Theresia caught a glimpse of something shiny, blending in with the black interior - his bow. She'd never truly cared enough about him to notice it before, when he'd opened it in the past.

Walter's eye caught hers, for a single second, as he turned to leave once again. He stopped. He stared. No one seemed to notice, not George, not the suspicious Tamanna, not Eden. He smiled, just a twitch, as if whatever -whatever it could be- Theresia suspected of him was true. Then he left.

Theresia turned to Eden. She felt the girl's hand touch hers. Their fingers interlaced. Eden's hand was pale and sweaty, as though it was covered in the same, cakey, suffocating makeup that her face was. Theresia looked into Eden's eyes, and saw again, those emotionless contact lenses. They covered so much of her eye that Theresia couldn't guess what the actual color was.

"I've been thinking," said Eden, a little smile forming on her face, "What do you think Walter tastes like?"

TAMANNA

When Armand didn't return with Walter, she should have realized something was wrong. Instead of feeling the sense of worry, the sense of needing to find out more, make sure the only person she remotely trusted was okay, she found herself inching towards Evangeline, scheming with Ilays, and feeling excited and happy with no need to get to school.

"So how are we bringing it up with her?" Ilays hissed.

"I have no actual clue." was Tamanna's best reply. "She doesn't remember anything, she's already said it before."

"Just pretend to return the letter, then kinda hint at the name?" Ilays suggested.

And so, it was settled. Tamanna was chosen to be the diplomat of the mission, considering it was she who had taken the letter from Evangeline, and she hadn't bothered the old woman with questions before.

Tamanna snuck up to Evangeline, who had just finished talking loudly and had started back to the bus. "Hi, Evangeline." The old woman turned. "Oh, hi, dear."

"I came to return your letter." Tamanna waved the piece of paper.

Evangeline smiled—a serene, old gummy expression—and took it back. Tamanna felt her heart physically wrench as the letter was pulled away from her fingertips.

"Also, you said you needed some help with something on your phone?"

"Ooh, yes, I do." Evangeline beckoned, and they hopped onto the bus and took a seat. The old woman took out her little box phone from her purse and turned it on. "My son-in-law's native language is Irish. I want to say hi to him in Irish, in the chatting app—what's that called? I think it'll make him happy. Can you help me do that?"

"Of course," Tamanna said warmly, and for a moment she nearly forgot why she needed to talk to Evangeline. What a fantastic mother-in-law she was.

Tamanna took the phone, and started to tinker with its settings. As she did, it dawned on her that she was on a mission, and so as nonchalantly as possible, without looking up from the device, she said, "I've been meaning to ask you something, Evangeline. About that letter?"

"Oh, yes, ask away." Evangeline smiled eagerly.

Tamanna swallowed. "Uh, well, I was reading that letter—fantastic letter, by the way. The penmanship was incredible. If you don't mind me asking, since we're all stuck here anyway, who is Nathan Colbert? I think I've heard the name before. And what was he talking about?"

That was a lie, of course. But she couldn't reveal what Ilays had shown her. Evangeline licked her lips. She stilled. "Hmm. Nathan Colbert. Where did you hear his name from?"

"He's the man that wrote the letter—"

"No, dear, I mean, you said you think you heard the name before. From where?"

Tamanna blinked. She looked up from the phone and into Evangeline's eyes, and those very eyes, clouded by cataract and dementia and a critical feature of the clueless expression the old woman always wore, were gone, and in their place was something sharp, something keen and waiting. Uncomfortably, Tamanna shifted and said carefully, "I'm not too sure, but he's familiar. Didn't he have something to do with…"

Time slowed. Her heart stopped racing. Thoughts sifted through her brain faster than they ever had before. *Nathan Colbert talked about watching Evangeline's performance. Evangeline's name is B. Joanna-Marie. B. Joanne- Marie is the author of the* Know Your True Worth *book.* Know Your True Worth *is a book about organ values.*

And time sped up again. Tamanna finished her sentence, almost out of breath, like she was finishing a race. "…Something about organs and such, I believe. He was a coroner, or a surgeon, I believe?"

The new, strange look in Evangeline's eyes flickered. The creases on her face deepened, like she was struggling, as though there was something she had not forgotten yet. All Tamanna felt in that unbearable moment of anticipation was a surprisingly deep guilt for causing that struggle in the old woman.

"Colbert…" Evangeline muttered. "He *is* a surgeon. How do you know?"

"I think he came up in my biomed course a while ago." this time, the lie rolled easily off Tamanna's guilty, guilty tongue. She watched Evangeline nod thoughtfully, far too keenly than she looked capable of. Finally, she spoke.

"Nathan… He was a good friend of mine, I think. I've had dementia for sixteen years now, and I haven't completely forgotten him, it seems." Evangeline smiled, a little sadly. "He never visited me in the residents' home."

"You both met in the medical field?" Tamanna guessed.

Evangeline nodded again. "Oh yes. He wrote me that letter, we met, and I took him under my wing, as my apprentice."

That means… Tamanna didn't have time to fully grasp the realization.

Evangeline continued, now a little quickly. "I was one of the only women in the field back then. When you look around yourself like that, wearing what everyone else thinks is a man's coat, doing what they think is a man's job… you get used to being the subject of contempt."

The subject of contempt. Something hit Tamanna inside. Evangeline sighed, and shook her head. "Nathan was different. Twenty years younger than me, had an older brother in the same department, one of those classic traditional men.

His brother must have said all those things about me, that I was a man of a woman, that I didn't belong there, and yet he never once thought of me as anything but his teacher, his helper. He wasn't like those other men."

Evangeline met her gaze, but it seemed like she couldn't actually see Tamanna. "You're a different girl, too, you know. You don't use phones like the other kids these days. You write—I bet your handwriting is good, too. You ask your elders for knowledge and advice. You help other people, you do volunteer and such. I have a feeling you'll be a fine woman one day, paving the way and breaking the rules and defying all the odds."

Tamanna was a smart girl. She'd been told something similar by many people. But it meant something different coming from Evangeline. She couldn't even believe she'd thought of the old woman as just some religious white oldie that probably baked the crumbliest muffins for her grandchildren. She hated to digress, seeing the faraway look in Evangeline's eyes — it was likely no one asked her this question in a long time — but she needed to know the truth.

"You said he was your apprentice? So, you were a surgeon too?"

"Oh, yes!" Evangeline was now delighted. "One of the finest. You know the Ortega Clinic and Hospital downtown? I was the reason they installed the operating theater in it, forty years ago. Interns and rookies would come watch me perform surgeries on my patients, and they'd learn from me… well, the ones that didn't have too much of an ego, anyway. That was where I met Nathan, too."

That checked out. Nathan had written in the letter of Evangeline's 'performance'. It was so incredibly difficult to wrap her head around the fact that Evangeline was once a skilled surgeon that had people watching her and calling her operations 'performances'. "That's incredible," Tamanna said, and this time, she didn't have to lie. "What type of a surgeon were you?"

"I was a general surgeon," Evangeline said, "But if I recall correctly, Nathan was in line to be a critical care surgeon. And he still came to me."

It was then that Tamanna, growing more and more suspicious, had to question - did Evangeline really have dementia at all? Tamanna had no idea how the disease worked, but it felt as though the old woman remembered quite a lot for someone who was sent to an old age home for not being able to remember anything. She couldn't even remember where she got her *Know Your True Value* book from. Tamanna didn't want to ask, though, for fear that it would be impolite.

"So, um, in the letter, though, Mr. Colbert addresses you as Joanna-Marie, or someone else," Tamanna pointed out, hoping she wasn't straining Evangeline's brittle brain that much. "That's not your name, though." she decided she could bring the book up later.

Evangeline blinked. "Hmm?"

"Your name, it's, ah, Evangeline, isn't it? Like the biblical…" The biblical something. Tamanna didn't know. "Mr Colbert wrote the letter to a B. Joanna- Marie. But you said he wrote it to you."

"Did I?"

Deep confusion creased Evangeline's already deeply lined face. "I don't think…" She sighed heavily and shook her head. "I don't… I'm not… sure?"

Maybe it was her ageing eyes that were wet, or perhaps new tears formed in those moist blue eyes. Evangeline struggled with herself, shaking her head, like she wanted to know, but she simply couldn't let it all go to dementia. Finally, she looked at Tamanna, sadly, and touched her little silver cross necklace.

"I don't know, dear," she admitted. "I think my age might have gotten to me."

"That's okay." Tamanna stopped herself from sighing in frustration. "You're so lovely to listen to, Evangeline. Maybe you could tell me some more stories about yourself sometime? Whatever you remember, of course."

"Of course," Evangeline gushed, and the disappointment disappeared from her face. "You go on the bus every day, don't you? Sit with me and I'll tell you everything this old gal remembers." she tapped her brain with a wrinkled finger.

"Thank you," Tamanna said, with as much sincerity as she possibly could.

She stood, and left the bus to join Ilays.

She couldn't see the struggle continue, in Evangeline's decaying brain.

ARMAND

The pain was still there when he woke up. Armand first opened his eyes from that abyss that consumed him, and the world around him, the world he saw sideways as he lay between grass blades — the dark green leaves, the shaded trees and grass, the quietly murmuring critters — seemed just are harsh and hurtful. His tracksuit jacket was entirely missing, and his bare torso was freckled with goosebumps and frosted in sweat. He had no idea how much time had passed. He felt his stomach growl. Slowly, over the course of hours and hours and hours, the pain twisted to take on the form of the hunger — as though whatever Walter had forced into him, whatever had held him prisoner and tortured him in that terrifying chasm, refused to let go.

Armand's head turned of its own accord, to a pile of food that lay on the forest bed just a little distance away from him. His hunger spoke in place of his senses, and with whatever energy he had — energy he didn't even know he possessed — he crawled to the food. Energy drinks, chips, protein shakes. Things he had refused before, back on the bus. But he didn't remember refusing it, and the mere thought of refusing food of any sort — if he had any thoughts left in him at all — was outrageous. Armand dragged himself to the nearest thing he could grab. His hand reached out desperately. It came in contact not with the cool plastic surface of a drink or crinkly packaging, but smooth, cold leather.

It was a little book. A little diary, just like the one Tamanna wrote in. That was what it looked like to Armand. And then it was all it looked like to him. He imagined it really was Tamanna's diary, and so he grabbed at it and flipped it open.

He saw what he thought Tamanna's handwriting would look like, and when he began to read the first page of the first entry, it was Tamanna's voice in his mind. But when he read the first paragraph—a little informational segment, like a column in a newspaper—all thoughts of the girl vanished.

First, there was a date. Three years and two months ago. Then there was a name. Female.

Then, in bulletin points, came the way she twitched with her eyes closed, exactly when she'd started sweating, and how she whimpered unconsciously.

Then came another date. Two years and eight months ago. There was another name. Female again.

Bulletin points, in the most beautifully authored, exquisitely penned writing, explained her exact rate of breathing over the course of an hour. Her fingers had moved of their own accord, apparently, and at one point, she had started to smile in her sleep.

Then came the next name, and the next and the next and the next, over the course of the next two and a half years. Each date came closer and closer to the present. Each person had reactions and descriptions and observations. Next to each and every name was a single red dot. Armand sat there, not a thought in his mind, not a drop of energy in his body, and read of how one girl had seizures and one man had skin rashes and another man had started to cry and another woman twitched her nose like a bunny. He flipped page after page and learned of people he never met. He learned more about them, he realized as he read on, than they knew about themselves.

The entries and the neat handwriting stopped abruptly a little less than halfway through the journal. The last entry was the present date.

There was a name. *Armand Ewing.* Male.

And then there was a description. Armand read of how he had trembled and collapsed, and of how he had no difficulty in breathing, and how he had cried like another girl had cried in the past, and how he had slipped into sleep. He read not only of his pulse and his heartbeat, like the others, but of how his muscles shifted, of what a hollow somewhere around his neck felt like, of the constituents of the grime under his fingernails. He read about himself in the light of someone else's eyes. He read about himself as though he had never met himself before.

Next to his name, he found once he finished reading, was a single yellow dot.

It seemed as though the pain that lingered snatched away his ability to use more than one sense at the time, because it was only after he finished comprehending the text he read that he heard the footsteps. Armand looked up, and found Walter staring down at him, so impossibly tall. The emotion on the coach's face was incomprehensible. Slung over his shoulder was his archery bag, and in his hand he held a plastic bag.

Walter noticed the book in Armand's hands. Not a trace of anger flickered through that mysterious expression as he crouched, gently peeled the journal away from Armand's sticky, awkward fingers, and tucked it away into his jacket. He lifted Armand's arm and dragged him away from the food—food only now Armand remembered he wished to eat—and propped him against a tree. Walter sifted through the plastic bag, and bought out a sandwich wrapped in plastic, a small bushel of grapes, and fruit juice. Not energy drinks, not protein shakes, not neon colored liquid that settled oddly in the stomach or made you stronger. Fresh fruit and sandwiches from a convenience store.

Walter smiled a little. "I went and told them we couldn't find the roads yet and so we were going back to search for them. You weren't awake when I came back the first time, so I decided to walk around a bit. Turns out the road's right around that bend over there, when you take a left at a fork." He gestured off somewhere, to a place Armand couldn't see. "I couldn't see any car services anywhere, which explains the driver being missing for so long. But then again," he smiled, "None of us seem to want to go home, now, do we?"

He sat back, apparently untroubled by Armand's lack of reply or reaction,

and placed the food before Armand. "I walked a bit and found a convenience store. There isn't too much out there. It isn't downtown or anything, just a suburb-like something. Dusty old town. But there was a store and it had food. Now all those idiots can choke on my students' protein shakes, while you get to have *these*. Isn't that cool? You're special. You are."

He talked like he would to a hyperactive six-year-old. Slow, gentle, and excited. Walter unwrapped the sandwich and placed it in Armand's hands. Those hands moved mechanically, from his lap to his mouth, and Armand, with not the energy or ability to run a thought through his head, ate. He ate mindlessly, pushing bread into his mouth and looking over at Walter and listening to him speak.

"Now, I know you might be worried or confused or whatever," said Walter casually. He sat cross-legged some distance away, and once the sandwich was finished, plucked grapes from their stems and handed them one by one to Armand. "I also know you found my journal. Double confusion. I get it. But I'm going to need you to put your confusion aside for a while. Once you're done eating, I'm going to ask you some questions, and you're going to answer them. Got it?"

Armand stared at him numbly. Walter plucked a grape, rubbed it clean on his shirt, then placed it on the peak of Armand's bent knee for him to eat. He had slowly begun to regain his senses, and though everything seemed addled and he still felt as though he was drowning in thick water, some of his thoughts had returned. And they all screamed at him to avoid whatever he'd done to feel that pain. Armand took the grape, put it in his mouth, and nodded. Walter smiled, satisfied. "Good. And I'm glad you know not to ask dumb questions like 'what if I don't?' because let's be honest, the last time you did that? Yeah… you get it."

He talked like he was talking to a normal person, a person he hadn't touched or hurt or threatened. Like he was talking to a friend. He carefully picked the bigger grapes out from the bushel, wiped them clean on his track suit, and carefully placed them where Armand, limbs still heavy, could easily reach it. Like he was caring for a sick friend.

A part of Armand told him to eat slowly and ignore the hunger, for he knew the era of peace and care and this bitter friendship between them would last only as long as the grapes kept coming, but his hunger clouded him even as his senses gradually returned, and before long, just as his judgement returned at long last, Walter placed the last of the grapes on his knee.

"Now you answer my questions, all nice and calm, and then we'll carry on, okay?" Walter pulled out the journal he had taken from Armand—the one that contained those awful, hidden secrets—and a pen and flipped it open., "I have a lot of things planned for you to do, and I know you'll do them all for me. You *will* do them all for me, won't you?" and then he smiled, because he knew Armand couldn't answer.

"Now clear your throat. Get your voice ready. Tell me what you felt the very moment you blacked out."

Pain, Armand wanted to say. Instead, he opened his mouth and the sounds that came out were, "What was it?"

Walter glanced up at him. "You answer my questions, I answer yours. Well, if I want to. What did you feel the moment you blacked out?"

"Pain."

"What sort of pain?"

"I don't know. All the sorts."

Walter took a moment to write it down. Armand noticed that he was writing from the back of the book, not somewhere in the middle from the start, where the descriptions and all the other people were. There was a whole different world Armand hadn't noticed. "All sorts of pain. Mental? Physical? Like a stab wound or an organ having trouble?"

"All of them."

"Did you see anything?" "Pain."

Walter stopped writing. He looked up, a frown creasing his eyebrows, as if he actually might be concerned. "What did it look like?"

"It was like sharp glass. Not like a broken mirror though, but like a crystal, sort of. I thought it was pretty, even when it hurt."

Walter touched the pen to the paper again, but didn't seem to write any of it down. He murmured, "That was a good sentence.

Cohesive. Alright. Did you feel nausea, or suffocation anytime throughout?"

"No."

"Did you feel anything else besides pain?" "No."

"Can you describe the pain in any detail?"

"No."

"Are you okay? You—"

Walter stopped mid-sentence and shook his head. His frown grew deeper. Whatever sympathy he seemed to have had been forced away. He murmured to himself, tapped his pen against his chin, then flipped back to the front of his journal where his victims and their reactions lay. It was only then that Armand realized—all the rest of them in the book had been given whatever Walter had forced into Armand. He was recording their reactions, what it did to their bodies. *A drug. A new drug.*

He wanted to ask what it was again. But he saw Walter stare at him, long and hard and so deep in thought that it felt as though if Armand said a single word, uttered a single syllable, Walter would snap out of his reverie and kill him in rage, like a dormant beast escaping hibernation, in search of its first meal. So, Armand stayed silent until Walter finally snapped the journal shut, scowling, and tucked it back into his pocket.

"Okay." Walter looked up at him with a glare. Then the glare softened, as if he was still holding on to that humanity. But then he seemingly let go of the emotion, for his gaze turned into something smoother, but just as sharp and sinister, a more quietly controlled rage. "Now, like I said before, you think something's wrong with Eden, and I saw Theresia kill that rabbit. I'm not going to do a thing about it, because I value my life. Yours, I value a little less. You're going to go spy on them for me."

Armand opened his mouth to protest. He valued his own life, probably more than Walter did. Walter raised his hand, and Armand decided against protesting.

Something clicked on in his brain, the little cop in him woke up leisurely, and told him that his life was risked just as much here, in a secluded forest with Walter, as it was between a critter killer and a possible murderer.

Walter seemed to understand the turmoil in Armand's head. He smiled.

"Keep my offer in mind—you do what I need you to do, and you don't feel pain. You can always refuse, of course, but not before I administer my second round…"

"What do you mean, *spy on them*?"

Walter's smile turned victorious. "We go back, tell them we don't meet the road for miles. Everything's normal. I'll keep talking around, keeping everyone calm—though it already feels like no one wants to go home now—and make sure no one else poses the threat of offing us, and you keep your eye on those two."

"And how will you make sure no one else poses the threat of *offing* us?"

Armand scoffed.

Walter shrugged. "I'll just have to poke at them. It'll be risky."

Armand rubbed his forehead. It still felt hollow. None of the former pain existed anymore, but the thought of it returning was enough to shake Armand's faith in everything that stood.

Armand's body told him firmly that it would kill itself before letting that pain return.

"Well?" Walter prodded. "What do you say?"

Like it was a business deal. He asked like Armand had a choice. Armand did the only thing he could — he nodded.

Walter smiled. "Good boy. Here. You like orange juice?"

Armand nodded.

THERESIA

It was when no one was watching that Eden started to get jittery. It had been long established that they could not sneak off into the forest for Eden to eat her fill of Ames whenever they wanted, but had to leave at carefully timed moments, with Theresia acing as a lookout to make sure no one ever noticed the disappearance.

But since she'd been caught, Eden hadn't had a chance to go back in the forest, for the moment Walter had left, all suspicious in his dark glances, George had called for everyone to come around so he could explain the situation to them. It seemed like the perfect time — in the midst of a good, lengthy lecture, no one would notice if Eden just snuck off. But there was no way that tall, keen, scarily observant hunk of a man that George was wouldn't notice if Eden was gone. So they stood together, squished between the teenager, Tamanna, and the annoyingly old Evangeline, as George explained how Walter and Armand would be back before the hour struck 11, and answered questions on what they could do once the two returned.

"I'm not really sure what we'd do if they found an exit, to be honest," George was saying. Theresia's gaze snagged to the road behind them — and two small figures advancing. Walter, with his bag slung over his shoulder, and this time, Armand was accompanying him. The police officer looked small and childish compared to the lithe, bear-like Walter; an especially clear difference when they wore the same style of tracksuit.

Unfortunately, others seemed to notice the two returning men as well.

Tamanna called out, excited, "Hey, look! They're back!" and nearly everyone turned to watch them, returning like heroes from a lost war. The tension in the air was tangible. It itched Theresia's skin and tickled the back of her ear as they all awaited the final truth—was there some hope yet? Could they walk back to civilization? Were they not so stranded after all? And Theresia could see it, too, in their eyes—Evangeline and her misty blue eyes, Ilays and Tamanna sharing the same expression of brown eyes full of hope, George with his apprehensive blue eyes contrasting his dark skin. Eden's fingers twitched in Theresia's palm. The girl looked annoyed. Theresia was too. If they could reach the road quickly, they would all go their separate ways. She would never see them again. Ames's corpse would be left unfinished. No one would ever know the truth. There was no fun in that.

Walter was the first to speak when they reached the bus. Something glinted in his eyes. His lips twitched. He fed on their collective impatience, their hopes, before sighing slowly and saying, "We walked for a good few miles. There's nothing but trees."

The wide blue sky seemed to collapse on their heads. The hope turned into a fragile mirror, lifted and shattered to the ground and becoming an omen of bad luck. Inside, Theresia rejoiced. She turned those shards into beautiful glittering things and celebrated for her future. She celebrated with Eden. Theresia looked over at the young woman and smiled silently.

"We yet live," whispered the girl, so quietly, that it was almost as if she had thought it and Theresia had read her mind. And all of a sudden, she did not seem like the same Eden anymore. She didn't sound like the swaying, energetic, stubborn creature she had been when she entered the bus and cracked her jokes, when she hunted down Ames and scavenged the rabbit behind the bus. She was Eden, the mistress of the garden, the careful watcher of the heavens, and Theresia felt the slow confirmation of her earlier realization—when it was all over, it would be revealed that they were never a team at all. It was Eden's game, and Theresia was the last of her prey. There was no special bond, there was no partnership.

Theresia would be hunted down like the rest of them. She would taste the same.

Inside, Theresia smiled. It was her game too. Eden's bones were only so strong.

Evangeline was the first to break the miserable silence. She grumbled something unintelligible and returned to the bus, as she had done far too often. What remained of their little group dissipated, slowly. Theresia watched discreetly as Walter caught Armand's arm, and spoke to him. His lips moved carefully, and he did not bend over to whisper into Armand's ear so as to not attract attention.

Armand replied in the same way, hesitantly pulling his arm away. His eyes shifted around faintly. He replied in return. Walter turned away, and Armand's body seemed to bristle tensely.

The young man waited for a while, crossing his arms, walked around a bit, then began to walk towards Theresia and Eden.

"I knew it," Theresia heard Eden whisper. She, too, knew. She let go of the girl's hand and walked to meet Armand.

"That's a shame, huh?" she said, when they collided. The young man nodded. "I tried staying hopeful when we were walking," he replied, "but after a while I guess we both knew. Who knows where the driver went off to.

Theresia nodded sympathetically, looking him over. He had entered the bus wearing a coat, a sweater over a collared shirt, trousers, and neat shoes. There had been a messenger bag over his right shoulder and a little yellow metal pin over his left breast pocket. He'd left his bag inside the bus, on the floor of his seat, and now he wore a tracksuit far too similar to the one Walter was wearing. Only the metal pin, some sort of emoji, remained from his former apparel. It clung to the sports fabric, blowing its sad little party popper.

Armand began to shift, as if he was going to walk away. "If you don't mind me asking," Theresia blurted. Armand turned back to her patiently. "Are those

Walter's clothes?"

A touch of color appeared in Armand's cheeks. "His student's, actually," he said. "He spilled energy drink on me a while ago."

"Oh. Good thing he had an extra, then, huh?" Theresia replied. "We're going to be here for a while, it seems."

And then it hit her—a sudden cruel inspiration, a gift for Eden, though she surely didn't deserve it. Trying not to smile, she continued, "I'm afraid people might not hold on for much longer. Not that they have any reason to."

"Hold on?" Armand prompted. Theresia shifted her gaze from the boy's face to the background, the scene behind his ear and temple. The bus lay still behind them. Standing at the back, where Theresia had caught the white rabbit, was Walter. From time to time, he glanced their way.

"I mean," Theresia said knowingly, "People like Evangeline are somewhat helpless. They'll wait until someone comes to rescue us, which is unlikely. But I'll bet in the next hour or so — by noon, at least, someone's going to get tired of waiting for no reason. They'll start walking, no matter what. Anything to get out of here after being stranded for what, a couple hours now?"

"Around two and half hours, yeah." an odd glint entered Armand's eyes, and he straightened. "Huh. I never thought of that. They *could* leave, couldn't they?"

"If they got sick enough of waiting, yeah."

Eden appeared at Theresia's side. "What are you both discussing so intensely?"

Armand licked his lips thoughtfully, staring at Eden. Theresia answered,

"Well, we were just talking about how, really, anyone could just walk out of here if they wanted. Couldn't they?"

Eden frowned deeply. "But they *wouldn't*," she replied, almost accusing Theresia silently of putting thoughts in Armand's head. "We promised we'd all stick together. Besides, Armand and Walter say even if there's civilization around, it's really far away, and people like you and me can't walk too long. What about that young girl there, with the glasses? What about the old woman? They can't walk at all, and we can't just leave them."

"No, we can't," Armand muttered, more to himself than them. Theresia exchanged a look with Eden — the man was definitely up to something. And Walter was surely involved.

Armand sent them a brief glance and a smile, then walked away, arms crossed. Eden and Theresia began to walk back to the bus, slowly. As they walked, Eden whispered, "The kid can't really hide his emotions, can he? Man gives away everything."

"Yeah, Walter's kind of dumb for that." Theresia watched him go back inside the bus.

"Hey, wait a minute." Eden stopped and looked over accusingly at Theresia. "What the hell was all that about? Why'd you tell him they could all just walk? We didn't agree on that."

"What are you going to do, eat everyone on the bus?" Theresia scoffed.

"No, but maybe just one more. I haven't done this in so long, you know. And besides, Ames was blackmailing her colleague. Who knows what everyone else has in them. Won't that be fun to find out?"

Theresia shrugged. "Don't worry, darling. I know what I'm doing. See, I figure, if we manage to form a group of three—you, me, maybe Armand, maybe the kid, maybe that Muslim girl, anyone. Three of us decide we're walking back to the road. We start walking. We get out of their sight, and it's just the two of us and an unsuspecting third party."

Eden blinked. Her jaw worked for a second, as if her teeth were anticipating biting into more flesh. "Wait. You did that for me?" Theresia nodded. "Well, duh. Who else?"

Eden grinned. "Oh. I like you, you know. Who are you thinking?"

"Walter's too big. What about Armand? He looks like he suspects us."

Eden wrinkled her nose. "But he's a cop. Wouldn't it be hilarious if we left him for last? A cop that couldn't even figure anything out? Besides, he's kinda sweet."

"He'll taste the same," Theresia reminded her. "Who else do you want?"

Eden thought. Then she sighed. "You're right. We need to get rid of someone who suspects us. And Walter's too big for you to kill. The cute guy it is."

They walked in silence until they reached the bus, and Eden climbed up the metal steps first. Theresia followed, muttering, "He's not that sweet, you know. He's just a kid."

Eden smiled brightly. "Still. He'll taste the same anyway."

ARMAND

Armand was sitting in his former seat on the bus. To the right, next to the window, his bag—which he had left on the floor, unprotected—snuggling in his lap. It all didn't exist. It all didn't happen. He stared out of the window, pretending the trees were screaming by, that they were on the road, at a signal, next to other cars, with their driver.

He had no idea if or when he'd fallen asleep, but in the blink of his eye, or perhaps slowly, he faded away and found himself in a dark room. The room was all too familiar, but he couldn't remember where he'd seen it. There was a single lightbulb flickering from the center of the ceiling. A little square mirror hung over a sink in the corner. Behind a plastic screen was a toilet, the ceramic cracking.

Armand sat in a corner, on a ragged quilt he somehow knew served as his bed.

He'd seen it before. He didn't know where. He'd seen it before, today, just as a little flash, somewhere in his world of pain, but he hadn't recognized it then. He knew the drug had brought it out of him, but he didn't know where it came from. Armand stood. The ground was closer to him than it usually was. He walked to the sink to wash his face. In the mirror, he appeared to himself as he might have been, years and years ago. *Eleven,* he remembered. The number came out of nowhere. But he knew it for certain—he was eleven years old.

Armand looked around the room once more, silently. He wanted to call out for help, ask if anyone was there, but something told him not to. Something told him he couldn't. Armand noticed a door in one of the walls. He started towards it. He touched the handle.

And then Armand was back on the bus. For a moment the bus was moving again, rolling down the road before taking a turn into the road in the forest. Then he collected himself, and the bus was no longer still driving. It slept still and dead in the middle of nowhere, surrounded by trees. Armand looked around, half-expecting to see the little prison room. But all he saw was seats and windows.

Evangeline slept soundly with her head against the rest of the seat in front of her, her purse tightly in her lap. Tamanna crouched next to her.

The girl slyly opened Evangeline's purse, and slipped her fingers in. She pulled the old woman's little phone out. Then she stood, turned, and found Armand staring at her.

"What are you doing?"

Tamanna grinned. "I know, I know. But you were really busy and Ilays and I are so close to figuring it all out. I swear, I just need some time."

Armand had no idea what she was talking about. He asked, "How long was I asleep for?"

Tamanna blinked. "I don't think… you weren't asleep. You were just staring out of the window all thoughtfully."

Then she slipped the phone into her pocket and hopped off the bus. Each of her steps down the three metal stairs clanked in Armand's brain, trying to form a headache. He watched her go. She had no idea of what was happening, did she?

She had no clue. Tamanna started to pace outside, fanning herself. Walter appeared from the hood of the bus, walking towards her. He stopped her. Armand straightened and watched them. He felt his face mechanically lean closer to the window, straining to hear their conversation, but he could only hear the wind, and see their lips move soundlessly. Walter caught Armand's gaze, uttered a final comment to the innocent Tamanna, and stomped inside the bus. His footsteps were irregularly harsh, as if he knew about Armand's headache and was trying to make it worse. He walked through the aisle, slowly, lumbering, like a predator toying with its next meal. Armand found himself wishing the man would sit somewhere else, but he knew what was to come.

Walter dumped himself next to Armand. Armand scooted aside, closer to the window, trying to maintain space. It felt as though he would remember those things again, the dark room and the pain, if Walter even so much as looked his way.

"Did you find anything?" Walter asked.

Armand scowled. "It's been like, a minute since we came back. Did *you* find anything?"

"No," Walter said. "But you were talking to those two. What did they say?" It took Armand a moment to realize he didn't remember the conversation, and another moment yet to remember once again. "They actually brought up a good point, I think. Theresia thinks that in a little while, there'll be people on the bus that will just get up and start walking to the road. They'll get tired of waiting."

"And what do you think about that?"

The question was so genuine that if anyone overheard, and didn't know any better, they would think Walter actually cared. Armand shook his head. "I think that when she said 'someone' she meant herself. Maybe she and Eden will start walking. Maybe they know we suspect them of... you know, everything, and they're going to escape."

"Hm." Walter rubbed his chin. "That's smart. You're good at putting together the clues, huh? No wonder you got promoted so easily."

It wasn't easy, Armand wanted to say. *So, stop talking about it.* He kept his mouth shut. The headache had disappeared, but he couldn't get that little room out of his head. It wasn't the fact that it existed; it was the fact that it had existed *before,* in his head. Where did it come from? It came from him. But it hadn't ever been there before. *It's the drug, the goddamn drug.* Whatever Walter had done to him, he could only hope it was worth it.

"You should stop hanging around me every five minutes," Armand managed finally. Rage seemed to seep into the cracks of his brain that the drug had torn open, and all of it was directed towards Walter. "People are going to get suspicious."

Walter only smiled, and crossed his arms. "You don't like me very much, do you?"

"Forgive me if I say I don't."

Walter stayed silent for a minute. He looked over at Armand. At some point, his gaze shifted from Armand's face to the window right behind him. "Theresia's staring at you," he murmured, his lips barely moving.

Armand didn't look. "Okay."

Walter cleared his throat. "Well, you have a job to do. I'll leave you alone." "Forever, I hope."

Walter only smirked. He got up, waved to Theresia, and left the bus yet again, to go talk to George. Theresia looked around - almost deliberately- walked over to the window and tapping the glass of his window. Armand looked down at her and smiled politely as if he hadn't seen her. Theresia glanced around again, then waved her fingers in a clear gesture - she wanted him to meet her outside the bus. Armand looked around, and back at her. She looked worried, almost. Armand sighed to himself, stood, stowing his messenger bag back under his seat, and joined her outside the bus.

The fresh air seemed to suddenly stop blowing around. It held its breath, waiting. Theresia took his arm discreetly, looking around, and pulled him to the backside of the bus, where no one could see them.

"What is it?" Armand asked. Theresia hadn't looked very worried the last time he talked to her, five minutes ago. And he hadn't seen her alone before. She was always with Eden. He looked down at his feet, saw the dark, fading stain of the rabbit's blood, and remembered Walter's words. Theresia had apparently killed the thing. *I don't want to end up like that rabbit,* Walter had said. As if Armand did indeed want to.

"No one's here, right?" Theresia muttered to herself, looking around. "Okay, good. I want to tell you something. Because you're a cop, you know, and… I don't know, I just trust you."

Only then did Armand actually remember he was a cop. He straightened, the way he always found himself straightening when he pulled a speeding car over and wrote them a ticket. "What is it? And where's Eden? I can't seem to find her anywhere."

"About her." Theresia glanced over at the forest. "You noticed it too, didn't you? She keeps going off into the forest."

He did. But for some reason, he didn't want to admit it to her.

"Armand, I followed her into the forest once. When you and Walter were out walking. I got suspicious when she went out once, after Ames went missing, and I saw her scarf stained red. With *blood*. I followed her, and she went all deep into the forest, on the other side, right into there-" she pointed, "and you wouldn't believe what I saw-"

She started to quiver. Her eyes filled with horror and tears the way they did before when she came out yelling about the rabbit. When she was lying. Theresia lifted a single finger, and beckoned for him to come closer. He did, half expected Eden to pop out from the forest, and hit him over the head with a log for his body to be dragged away and disposed of.

Theresia whispered, in a shaking voice,

"I found Ames."

"Where is she? Is she okay?" "She's dead-"

Armand closed his eyes.

"-And Eden was *eating* her corpse."

THERESIA

He believed it immediately. Theresia herself never considered herself more of the convincing types, but he believed it immediately. The officer didn't say anything, but Theresia could tell by the shift in his hazel eyes. His hand lifted up so quickly that Theresia nearly flinched, but it stopped near his chin. His fingers covered his mouth, almost thoughtfully. He stared down at his feet for a long time. After what seemed like forever, he looked back at her. The man was easily a head taller than her, but it still seemed like he was looking up to stare into her eyes, disbelieving.

Finally, he asked, in a slow, tempered voice, "Why are you telling me this?"

Theresia nearly forgot she had a facade to maintain. "I- I told you. You're a cop. I didn't know who else to tell, to trust. I don't know what to do."

Armand nodded. "How did you get back safely? Do you think she saw you?"

Theresia sniffed and shrugged. "I don't know. I'm scared. That poor, *poor* model. What if I end up like that or something?" She trailed off, and waited for him to react. He touched her shoulder sympathetically.

"Don't worry." he sounded so sincere. "I... I'm not sure what we can do. But if you're right, if what you saw was really what you think was happening-"

"It was.

"Then, I don't know how we'd handle that. But I promise I won't let her touch you."

"Thank you." Theresia wiped her eyes, and even she was secretly surprised to find her fingers wet. "I - Thank you. That means a lot. I have kids that are waiting for me, you know. You have kids?"

Armand's expression warped. His brows knitted. It was a subtle change, and it came in a thunderclap, disappearing as soon as it appeared, but Theresia noticed it. She wouldn't have, if she hadn't been staring insincerely into his face. Before she could think about it, he responded, "No."

"Well, I hope you'll understand me anyway. My children, they need someone to take care of them."

Armand nodded. He worked his jaw for a bit. "Do you have any thoughts?" he asked.

"What do you mean?"

"Do you think there's something we should do in particular? Do you have any thoughts on how to proceed?"

She knew. Theresia swallowed. "I..."

Armand nodded, understanding. He rubbed her shoulder again. "I'll protect you, I promise. I need some time to think out our next steps."

"Of course." Theresia watched him walk away. "Wait."

He turned. There was so much emotion on his face, and one of those emotions was clear-cut determination and concern - he would protect her, no matter what. Theresia almost smiled.

"Thank you," she said, and she had no idea if it was actually genuine. "For letting me trust you."

"Thank *you*," Armand said, "For trusting me."

He walked around the bus again. He would tell Walter, surely. Theresia smiled.

A moment later, Eden walked out from the forest. She stared at the spot Armand had been standing. "I thought you'd just tell him about the scarf, and nothing else. An eager girl, huh?"

Theresia shrugged. "You wanted them to know, didn't you?"

Eden shrugged. "Eh. I did, didn't I? That's on me, I guess." She wiped her hands on her striped sweater. "It's awfully nice of you to go through all that for me, though. That acting? Damn. Oscar-worthy, you know? Thanks."

Theresia smiled. "We're kindred spirits after all, aren't we?"

"Probably." Eden returned the smile. "Thank you," she said again, and walked past Theresia to the front of the bus. Theresia watched her go. Her smile grew.

If only Eden knew.

"Thank *you*," Theresia whispered. "Thank you, darling."

ARMAND

Armand didn't move from the seat. His wristwatch passed eleven-thirty am. He felt so comfortable sitting that he couldn't possibly imagine that he'd actually gotten out of it to hear Theresia's words.

I should tell Walter. He didn't want to. Walter didn't deserve it. But he had to. If Eden -and if Theresia was even right at all- knew that Armand knew, she'd be set on killing him. And if Armand told Walter what Theresia had told him, and if he believed that Eden had actually killed and *eaten* Ames, he'd be set on killing her. It was the safest option to tell Walter what he knew, before Eden figured out her secret was discovered. Walter could possibly kill Eden before the woman killed Armand -and ate him- or perhaps, since Armand was the unfortunately fortunate victim of Walter's experiments, he would be protected.

Armand wanted to get out of his seat and warn Walter, this man that had brought back the dark room and all that pain and beckoned the storm that raged in Armand's mind. But he couldn't. He couldn't move. His head had begun to pound again, this time harder than before, and it felt like it wouldn't go away. Armand inhaled as deeply as he could, and pressed his thumb against his temple, squeezing his eyes shut. The moment his vision turned into darkness, the room returned. The light bulb. The mattress. The locked doorknob. The sink. The mirror that showed him his true, eleven-year old self. It was so real, even though he had only closed his eyes, that Armand was afraid that when his eyes opened again, he would still only see that.

Then he began to hear voices. They were faint, and they came from outside the room. A female voice. A male voice. Whispering, laughing, talking, yelling.

Names popped into Armand's head. *Jabari.* The male voice. *Masika.* The female. He knew those names too well, and at the same time he had no idea who they were.

And then it all went away. Armand saw the darkness of his eigengrau again, the swirling blue and brown and orange with little flecks of light and color. A single face appeared in his mind, not as clear as his vision of the room but this time, he knew who it was. His boss, the man that had gotten him his promotion, a man who was almost his second father, or even his first - Captain Dwight Romero. Armand had always been closing to his boss - *but why do I see him now?* What did he have to do with the dark room? He hadn't put him there. Armand didn't know for sure, but he could feel it.

There was a tapping on Captain Romero's shoulder. A thick, muscular finger, tap-tap-tapping on the man's uniformed shoulder. Then the tapping transferred itself to Armand's shoulder, and he was once again on the cursed pink bus. The finger was now a hand, slapping his shoulder harshly, expectantly. The hand was Walter's. It never was anyone else's. Armand looked up at him, then scooted over. Walter sat next to him.

"I told you, you shouldn't keep sitting next to me like that." Armand was surprised that he actually could talk, still, instead of leaping right up and punching the coach. "People are going to get suspicious-"

"What did Theresia want?"

He thought about it again. It had flitted past him the first time she'd said it, and since, it had been a blur. He'd promised to keep her safe, to protect the woman as she cried and whispered terrified words. But if Eden really did *eat* Ames, if she was actually a cannibal, then how could Armand protect her, if they were all only flesh? Armand imagined for a second, Ames's carcass, her tall body, her perfect skin - but now that tall body was broken, and the perfect skin was marred, torn apart, white skin ripped off to expose her human flesh. She'd never abandoned them at all.

They'd abandoned her.

"I asked, what did Theresia want?"

Armand swallowed dryly. "Theresia told me…" "Told you *what?*"

"She told me that - that Eden…"

"What about Eden?" Walter hissed impatiently.

"She *ate* Ames, okay?" Armand spat, before lowering his voice. "Theresia told me she's a cannibal! She saw the blood on Eden's scarf, like I did, and followed Eden into the forest, and saw -actually *saw*- Ames's corpse, and she saw Eden eating it. And she doesn't know if Eden saw her, and she's scared for her life."

Walter froze. Armand knew the feeling he was going through right now - the absolute horror, the sudden chills, the beads of sudden sweat, the cold blood, the weak legs. He'd felt it all a moment ago.

"She what?"

Armand didn't answer. It wouldn't help. He waited patiently, blankly, until Walter came to his senses. His eyes fluttered. His jaw worked. He swallowed. He shifted in his seat, almost closer to Armand, as if he was scared to be alone, or alone with Eden. Then he looked over, and asked quietly, "Why did she tell you?"

"Huh?"

"Why would Theresia tell you that? The two of them are always together, aren't they?"

Armand nodded slowly. "Yeah. It's like they're friends, kind of. So why would she tell me that? Unless she didn't know about Eden until now, or…" "Or this is their plan."

Walter's voice was even. Armand hadn't considered the possibility before, and he didn't know if it was even possible. It was easy enough to surmise, but Armand had seen Theresia's face when she told him. He'd seen her tears and heard her trembling voice when she told him how she'd seen Eden eat Ames's corpse. It was too believable.

"Well, what do I do?" Armand asked quietly. "What if she asks me to confront Eden or something? If I don't go, they're going get even more suspicious. They might even do something rash. If I do go, and Eden is actually a cannibal, there's too much of a chance that I'll die."

"Aren't you an officer?" Walter said casually. "You're putting your life on the line for a civilian. This is just your duty."

Armand looked up at the cool calculation in Walter's eyes - so laconic, even when contemplating someone's death. The way a man who had witnessed many deaths would behave. The way Eden would behave, no doubt. He imagined himself grabbing Walter's arm, snapping off each finger, ripping the hair off the man's balding head, sinking his fingers into those brown eyes, peeling his lips off his face. He took in a deep breath, and met Walter's gaze calmly. "Now, now. Let's not act like I'm dispensable, okay?" There was almost a flicker of surprise on Walter's face.

"You know you can't let me die, don't you?" Armand continued softly. "I'm your experiment. I'm not just an experiment, I'm your special case. You think I didn't notice anything when I read your journal? You think I don't know that every single one of your test subjects died, until now, until me?" even as he spoke, he remembered clearly, the little red dots after every name in the journal, and the yellow dot next to his own. "You can't kill me, because I'm the only thing giving your drug a chance. You can't just not leave me to die, you have to *protect* me from Eden."

Walter scoffed. "So, you're smart, too. No wonder they made you a detective."

The room popped right back into Armand's head. This was the second time Walter said that. He wanted to tell the man to stop. He stayed quiet, like he seemed to be doing far too often, as Walter contemplated. The man rubbed his temples, then finally said, "the first thing we need to do, before anything else, is find out if it's true or not."

"Yes." Armand felt queasy again, all of a sudden.

Walter turned to him with an odd smile. "You. You're going to ask Theresia to take you to the body."

"What?"

"She said she saw Ames's corpse, half-eaten. Tell her to take you there, see the body for yourself, then come back and if she's right about Eden, we'll act accordingly."

Act accordingly. Armand would have scoffed. "Are you crazy? What if it's a trap? What if Eden's waiting for me there?"

Walter shifted his jaw. It felt as though he almost wanted to call Armand dispensable again, but he knew he couldn't. Finally, he said, "We'll need to work out a system. Run back the moment you think something's off."

"I think everything about this is off," Armand snapped. "For all I know, Theresia only told me because you're too big to kill and eat."

A ghost of a smile appeared on Walter's face. "You have your phone?"

"No. It got ruined when you threw Gatorade on it. You probably did that on purpose, too."

"Nah, man, that was an actual mistake. Get a phone from your friend, that little Indian girl. I'll give you my number. The moment you call I'll be there, if anything goes wrong."

Armand needed to argue that Ames being eaten was fundamentally wrong, but the moment he'd proclaimed it -that chances were, he was only being lured in because Walter wasn't easy to lure in- he knew it was true, and that made him so indescribably outraged that it made him sad. He wanted to grab his bag, take Tamanna and Evangeline, the only two innocent souls on this bus, and run away with them to the main roads Walter claimed were so close by.

That-

That's a fantastic idea.

GEORGE

George Torres knew something was wrong the moment he set foot on the crumbling tar ground, and walked out to face the steaming organs of the bus. Then the red headed woman went missing. He was only little less than absolutely sure when Walter, the archery coach, and Armand, the claimed police officer, went off to find a road together, and came back with no sight of anything but trees. It wasn't the fact that they went together that aroused his suspicions at first, but the way they didn't find anything after half an hour… that was, until George turned, and saw them walking off, slowly turning smaller and smaller - and Walter put an arm around Armand. When had the two become so chummy? After the single time they had talked, moments before they decided to walk off?

They returned unsuccessful, and that sealed the deal. George knew something was utterly fishy. Fishier than an ocean full of fish. George swore to himself that he would keep the two—especially Walter—at arm's length at all times. It made him wonder, with the way Walter looked around with those beady eyes of his, and it was not too hard to wonder, with the sheer size and strength he knew Walter possessed as a gym coach, if the man had anything to do with the poor model's disappearance. He could have killed her. But for what? He could have raped her, and then killed her. But then what was with him and the cop? They were surely in it together. Maybe they both had a hand in killing Ames. But

Armand didn't look the type to kill people. But he was a cop. And he could be a dirty cop.

George thought about it for a long time. He remembered to think about it more whenever he saw those two. It did him well, being suspicious, at work and in life.

George found himself watching Walter again from a distance. He stood close to the hood of the bus. He had been standing there since the damned thing broke down, for two reasons, mainly. One: he'd been trying to assess what really went wrong with it all day, for hours now. But he couldn't find anything wrong. He was a car salesman, not a repairman. His second reason was more of a recent development - standing at the very front of the bus gave him a good view of the rest of the scene, from the people actually sitting in the bus to those milling out and around it. His only blindspots were the back of the bus and the right side. He'd know whenever Walter disappeared to the back, and could act then.

When George caught himself scheming about this for the first time, he'd almost been appalled. *I've really come to this. On a stinking, run-down, pink-ass bus, spying on an archery coach and his little police sidekick that could probably find a way to put me in jail if he found out.* And it wasn't like George had nothing to hide, either.

Armand sat inside the bus, and Walter joined him. The two talked for quite some time, almost heatedly. Then the young woman, who usually lugged her stroller around -Theresia, he remembered- walked out from the back of the bus.

She spent quite a lot of time there, and George narrowed it down to the darned rabbit they'd run over. She'd been the most distraught. He didn't pay too much attention to her, until she stopped at the window of the seat Armand and Walter sat in, and began to talk with them. Her voice was soft and strained, and George couldn't hear a thing. Armand left the bus. He didn't notice George watching, as he followed the woman behind the bus. George looked down at his phone. He was in half the mind to simply call emergency services, get a tow truck, and hitch a ride away to his work, but he couldn't anymore. He was too late. He was too deep in it.

And besides, he was a salesman. He never had so much fun.

George nearly followed the two to his blind spot, or at least to another area of the bus to eavesdrop, but as he was contemplating it, Walter hopped off the bus. He sent George a quick, simple headnod, then began to walk back and forth, from one side of the road, across to the other. Moments later, Armand returned. As he got closer, George noticed the creases cutting across his forehead, and the frown knitting his eyebrows. He got back onto the bus again, and took his usual spot.

Like a machine, with a routine, going back and forth and back and forth.

George then felt his foot shift. He wanted to start a conversation, and ask the cop what was bothering him - it was incredibly clear that something was. But just as he took a step forward, Walter noticed his new friend was back in the bus, and hastily walked back. Ilays and Tamanna were out sitting on the side of the road, talking to each other, oblivious to the clear scheme that was playing out. Theresia walked out from behind the bus. She took a moment to look over at Armand from the window, then went back to her usual place where the rabbit had been killed. He saw her shadow from behind the pink monstrosity, and figured she was resting.

Eden was probably around there as well, considering the two of them spent much time together. And for the first time since the snacks had been distributed, Evangeline was out walking up and down the road with her hands clasped behind her back and her giant handbag presumably back in her seat.

No one was watching old George.

George slowly began to pace. He could hear Walter and Armand hissing to each other. He edged closer.

"Told you..." Walter murmured.

George took two steps forward, ensuring his figure would be covered by the metal frame of the window, and that he'd remain unseen. "Told me... Eden..." Armand mumbled.

George's feet whispered as he walked forward, this time with a clever leap to hide from Walter's view behind Armand's head. "Told you what?" Walter snapped.

And then said Armand,

"She ate Ames, okay? Theresia told me she's a cannibal!"

George lingered moments later. He missed the conversation. His ears bloated in and out of their hearing. It wasn't only the unspeakable fact he'd heard, or the danger he now knew he was in, but the eerily calm tone in which Armand and Walter continued to discuss their plan of action. There was something about confirmation, finding a corpse. There were snide tones, smug words, scoffs and even the hint of a chuckle. *Chuckling,* after knowing that one among them ate people. As if they were used to it, or as if they were worse.

George thought, long and hard for a moment, about the thunderclap of a problem at hand. And then, he realized, he had the solution.

Walter was an archery coach. He had a bow, and arrows.

EVANGELINE

Nathan Colbert.

Six feet tall. Softly rounding jaw. Blue eyes. Dark blonde hair. Crew cut.

Only wore v-necked shirts when he wore his white coat. Cared for his nails.

Evangeline had been diagnosed with dementia when she was fifty-four.

Of course, she had started to slowly lose her memory before, but once the statement was made by a doctor—a doctor, like a doctor that she was, wearing the same coat that she used to, with the same expression she'd have—it seemed to Evangeline like the true and final moment her memories wouldn't come back once they left, as if before that statement was made, they were only temporarily gone, and they would come back soon. As the younger people said nowadays, they went to get the milk.

Over the course of the next sixteen years, Evangeline slowly forgot everything. She thought it would make her feel peaceful, to put aside everything that happened in her hectic career once and for all, and forget the guilt and stress and the feeling of her fingers trembling in an operating theater with a hundred people watching, but when she did forget, she felt as though a part of her chipped away. She was an ageing cement pot that was worn away with use, that couldn't be brought back, that couldn't be fixed once it fell and shattered. When she reflected within herself, only a few years ago, she couldn't remember the name of her son- in-law. She knew him. She talked to him. But somehow, every time she left her daughter's house, she would simply forget the man's face and his name and how he spoke. She could no longer remember any of the memorable patients she worked with, what her boss spoke like, who she interned with, or what her late husband's face looked like. She remembered the looks men had given her, a lady doctor, and the sexist remarks, and she remembered she was a general surgeon, though it was a real surprise she hadn't forgotten yet.

And then there was Nathan. She'd kept his letter in her purse for years, and she'd forgotten him. He'd written that to her when she was forty. He was twenty- five years old, a young man in medical school, who wished to intern for her. She hadn't noticed him when she'd performed the surgery he wrote of in the letter, but after she met him, in a little coffee shop close to his cosy suburban home, he was the only reason she performed her surgeries. For a long while, at least.

Evangeline wasn't in love, no. She felt something even more precious for him - respect. There was respect between them, and understanding, something that could not be tarnished by a petty thing like love.

All of this... almost all of it she had forgotten. She had forgotten Nathan Colbert. She had forgotten what he looked like, what he spoke like, the look of awe on his face during every surgery of hers he watched. She'd forgotten it all, even with his letter in her purse for decades. And now, that sweet young girl had awakened something in her dying, sleeping brain, and Evangeline had begun to remember.

She felt as though there was something, something crucial to Nathan Colbert that she needed to remember, but couldn't. There was something she desperately needed to bring back to do this memory of him justice. She tried to remember with all her might, and yet it slipped from her grasp like everything did —

like her husband's face and her son-in-law's kind words and her caretaker's warnings.

Evangeline had come to accept those things she could not reach, even if it was only a step away. But she couldn't accept this.

She needed to remember Nathan. She needed to remember everything.

When the young girl with the glasses — Evangeline could never remember her name — left, after awakening those memories, Evangeline had tried to deny the newfound obsession. She tried to nap it off; that usually worked when she didn't want it to. Then she tried to walk, get some fresh air, but at an age like hers, arthritis was always awaiting a chance to leap, and so she needed to come back to her seat. That left her sweating and hungry, but she had no food.

In a desperate attempt to let her frail old mind rest with some nourishment, Evangeline hunched over at the bus's open door and called out, "Walter, young man!"

He wasn't young compared to some of the other people on the bus, of course, being a man well into his forties, but to Evangeline, they were all young. *Would he be as old as Nathan now?*

Walter, the young man, was standing outside impatiently. His eyes were trained keenly on his police friend, who stood out talking quietly to the nice young lady Evangeline had just been talking to. Evangeline called him again, then asked, "Would you be so kind as to direct me to some more food, if there is any?"

Walter did not seem interested in passing it out himself, as he did before. Instead, he pulled his long gym back off his shoulder and held it out. "Be careful, ma'am. I'm sure there's something inside."

"Thank you, young man. Should I…"

"Yes, yes, you can just place it on the seat there where I was sitting. I'll fetch it later."

"God bless you, yes sir."

Saying *God bless you* to everyone was arguably what made Evangeline feel the oldest. It never stopped her from saying it, though. God indeed did bless those that were kind at heart. Evangeline took the bag with some difficulty, then dragged it inside to her seat. She unzipped the heavy sack, sitting down. It was black and made of sports material. Inside was the long, sleek bow, and a set of arrows in a plastic cover. Walter happened to coach in archery, she knew, but the bow itself surprised her. The weapons had looked very different back when she was a child, and it looked nothing at all like those from the olden movies. She cursed the bland modern design for ruining a traditional appearance, as modernity always did, and sifted through the rest of the bag's contents. It was a horribly kept bow, especially for a coach. She didn't know much about sports in general, but she was sure it was stupid to put food and sports drinks in the same bag as one's instruments.

At the very bottom was a protein shake. It was chocolate in flavor but didn't taste much like chocolate at all. Evangeline had it twice before. They'd given it to her, guessing she required the most sustenance as an old person. They weren't too wrong. Evangeline took the milkshake out.

Then she noticed the several extra zips. Some were very obscure, like they were meant to hold only the most important things. Evangeline looked up and out. She couldn't see Walter. It was likely that Walter couldn't see her either. She looked back down at the bag. Something tingled inside her. The lost youth that had been washed away by her disease and age started to resurface again. *Why not,* she reasoned, *when he'll never know at all? He won't be able to tell. I won't move a thing.*

She began to reason with herself. Then she stopped reasoning. *Oh, I'm an old woman. I could kick the bucket tomorrow, or on this very bus. I can do what I want.*

Evangeline did so love being old sometimes. She put aside her rations, and began to open zips. Pens and pencils, a long black charger for an absent device, an old scented Chapstick. A little plastic bag–

A little plastic bag, with three small red pills in it.

If it weren't for the girl that had reminded her, Evangeline wouldn't have cared. But she wasn't just old, senile Evangeline now – she was Evangeline, the retired doctor. And those didn't look like medication.

Beside the baggie was a cloth. It was a handkerchief, folded multiple times to form a square. One side of it was soaked red. Evangeline's mind leapt to blood, first, but she touched it, felt it, and took the slightest whiff, and she knew at once it was the remnants of one of the red pills, perhaps mixed into something. But what was it?

Without thinking, Evangeline took the cloth in her hands. She bent down to meet it, instead of bringing it out of the bag to her face, and smelled it. She inhaled deeply, like she was a starved boy outside an eatery, or a poor man outside a gold shop. She knew she shouldn't have immediately; she didn't know what the pills were, why they were in Walter's bag, and what they could do to her. But she did it anyway. Then she closed all the zips of the bag, and tossed it to the seat beside her.

Evangeline felt the effects immediately. As she struggled to grasp what they were, and what it was doing to her mind and body, she hardly noticed the handsome, well-dressed George enter the bus. She didn't see him eye her suspiciously. She almost didn't hear him ask, "Ma'am, you wouldn't happen to be using that bag, would you?"

Evangeline rested her head on the backrest of the seat. She felt for the milk shake, then waved it before him - or wherever he was. "I suggest you get some rest yourself, young man," she said, or maybe she didn't. George took the bag and quietly left, looking about him suspiciously, but Evangeline never noticed. She knew at once she never should have touched those pills, or that kerchief. She was done for. The new feeling would spread all around her senses faster and faster, and that would be the only and the last thing she felt.

You said it yourself, Joanna, she told herself, breathing rhythmically. *You could die on this bus right here, right now. You're an old, old woman. You can do whatever you want.*

TWO YEARS AGO

Coaches and teachers weren't paid very well. They weren't too respected, especially teachers. There weren't many perks to a life of sharing knowledge, and certainly none the common people could think of, other than satisfaction or gratification. But there was one, one uncommon, odd little perk. You got to see an empty classroom, an empty dojo, an empty gym. And there wasn't anything

stranger, in Walter Lynch's opinion, than seeing a room that should be so full of loud people be completely empty. His favorite thing to do was to go around the class and touch everything that the kids used, every practice bow, every spare arrow, every target, the floor, the walls, the water fountain, everything, with a finger, and simply savor the emptiness.

Walter Lynch was once a very simple man. He'd go to the training center, in the giant fitness campus in the suburbs, check his mail, plan up the daily schedule, and enjoy the silence and peace until students came in. After attendance, they'd get to work. Naturally, they would be grouped into different levels, and Walter and his assistants and co-teachers would handle each one. Walter taught pros, the ones that looked like they could get into the Olympics or become coaches themselves.

Students would come and go, Walter would teach, plan, mark attendance, talk, help, and the cycle would continue until finally, as evening set, the last of the students would stream out, his colleagues would say goodbye, and Walter would be left alone in a great big arena with no one but himself. He would pack everything up and enjoy the peace again. To him, the post-class silence was far better than the pre-class silence, because there wasn't any anticipation of students coming in and ruining it all. It was just him, and no one else.

Walter would then pack up, lock the doors, and go to his apartment on his motorcycle. Sometimes he'd pick a little something for himself from a convenience store on the way. But either way, he always ate dinner alone. He slept alone. When he woke up, he was alone.

It wasn't like that anymore. His house wasn't empty. The little apartment meant for one was now for two, with a third constant guest - who fortunately, wasn't present now.

The moment Walter opened his door, he heard the giggling. Immediately, he dumped his belongings on the floor, and ran to the bedroom.

A woman lay spread-eagled on the bed, creating imaginary snow angels. A peal of laughter escaped her lips. Her skin was dry and cracked and her hair hadn't been washed in two weeks. She looked on the brink of death, and she probably was, but to her, it didn't matter. She was six years old and playing in the snow with her dog. That was what she told him.

Walter sat next to her on the bed and put his hand over her forehead.

Concern filled him; not for her, but for himself. This was the third attempt. He couldn't be allowed many more. "How are you?"

"I'm on my fourth angel!" she laughed. "Daddy's angels have bigger wings than mine and it's not fair!"

"Yes, yes. Do you feel well?"

"Yeah!"

Walter sighed. He pulled out a thermometer and checked her temperature.

104. He watched her longer, wondering when her family would start to notice her absence. She rolled around a bit more, then suddenly winced. The smile on her face disappeared. Walter whipped out his journal and furiously scribbled: *More headaches. Pulled back into the present. 104°F* . Her headaches were increasing. She was returning less. He watched her carefully, feeling something like rue. She smiled and moaned and grumbled, then began to laugh.

Walter flinched. He closed his eyes.

She laughed maniacally, gleefully. She clapped her hands and wiggled her fingers and toes and latched onto Walter's forearm with her hand and shook him and refused to let go. She laughed and laughed and played in the snow and remembered all the good times until the good times stabbed her in the back and made her foam at the mouth and made her eyes roll back in her head and flicker and empty out. She stopped laughing. She went still. She returned to the present for a single, tortured moment, turning from the little happy child in the snow back into his colleague, a talented, promising, determined young woman. The archer returned to her body, only to take a single, final breath, look around, and steal her life away.

Walter sat there for several seconds. Then he opened his journal, pulled out a red-capped marker, and placed a single round dot of red next to the woman's name. He turned back the pages, looking through his old writing. The last one had taken a month to die. She'd taken only two weeks.

Perhaps it was some sort of resignation to the miserable thing that had become his life, but in the end, Walter hardly needed any time to compose himself. He tucked away his red ink and his cursed journal, and looked over at the woman's face.

"Where will I find a replacement for you now?" he asked. She didn't respond, of course. He shook his head. "Shame. The kids really liked you. What was the point of it all anyway? You're dead. I'll be, too. It just won't work."

He stood up and left the bedroom, closing the door behind him gently.

"That one didn't sound like a success."

Walter turned. He'd forgotten to lock his front door when he came in. His frequent guest had welcomed himself in. Walter stared hard at the man in the suit. Frail, maybe a few inches over five and a half feet, and slightly potbellied, but not strong. He was younger than Walter, in his mid-thirties, and twice as cocky. He was so easy to kill, and yet he had all the power in the world.

"What do you want, Crane?" Walter sighed. He collapsed onto the sofa. The man sat next to him. Crane was definitely not his real name, but Walter would never know.

"She's dead, isn't she?" Crane asked. "Yeah."

"How long did this one take? A week and a half?" "Two. Two weeks."

"It's getting worse, then." "Yeah."

"Maybe if you decrease the dosage?"

Walter blinked. It wasn't like Crane to give him suggestions. "Then it isn't addictive at all if they take too little, and my guy at the lab says the main problem is the properties of the ingredients."

"But you can't take any of the ingredients out. It ruins the effects." "Yeah."

Crane thought for a moment. "That won't do at all, then. I mean *yeah*, drugs kill you, but no one's going to take a pill that offs them in two weeks. And it's been getting quicker and quicker, too. How does it even get quicker?"

"I've been trying to switch the synthetic ingredients up a bit, to increase the longevity. Most of them haven't been reacting well with the plant-based stuff."

"Right. So, one type could damage the brain faster, resulting in a quicker death, and the others give you too many migraines and such to be effective?" "Yeah, pretty much."

"Stop doing that, then."

Walter sighed. "I *can't*. If I go back to the first type, it'll only last a month. I can't find anything similar to it, that's suitable. This one's got me."

"Man, all I can say is that you have to think up of something fast." Crane grew serious. "The boss man needs his money. It's been three months."

"I'm trying, I swear," Walter mumbled. "I feel like I'm so close. I'll get it. I'll get something for you guys to put into the market, I promise. I just need more time."

Crane answered, "I don't know if you'll get it."

***

PRESENT

"I got her phone."

Armand was waiting for him on the other side of the bus, the one closer to the forest and less open to the eye. He held up a sleek phone. "She gave me her phone. What's your number?"

Walter gave it to him. "How did you get it? She couldn't have just given it to you." He knew this. She'd been roaming around with the Muslim girl, giving everyone creepy glances like some private eye. There was no way she wouldn't suspect anything, and there was no way Armand was brave enough to tell her anything. He wouldn't want her to get in trouble.

Armand shrugged meagerly. "I told her that my phone got ruined, which it did, technically. And that I needed a phone so you could send me pictures of some of your students that you thought were engaging in illegal activity. I told her I'd send it to myself and then delete it from her phone, quickly and easily."

"Smart boy." Walter hadn't much of an impression of Armand when the bus had first broken down, before everything had hit the fan, but as he spent more time with the man, he'd realized why Armand had decided to become a cop. Armand Ewing had wits and thought on his feet well. He was also smart and practical and knew when to do what. He was just a really bad liar. "Great, you have my number now. All you have to do is ask Theresia to take you to the body and determine for yourself if she's right or not. At any sign of danger, send me a missed call and try and get out of there immediately."

"And what will *you* do, if she has a weapon or something?" Armand asked, almost resentfully.

Walter thought for a moment. He really would have no problem subduing Theresia or Eden or even both if he had to, but if they really did have a weapon, which they surely did have — even if it was only a pocket knife or something — then Walter was just a mortal. "You're right. I'll keep my bag with me. I can stab them with arrows, if worse comes to worst."

"How relieving," Armand replied dryly. For a moment, Walter wanted to tear the man's neck off. He controlled himself.

"Before we do this, however, I need to ask you some things," said Walter, instead of loosing a yell and snapping some bones. He patted his pockets for his journal, before remembering he'd left it in his bag. Oh, well. "The aftermath. Have you gotten any memories, have you seen anything? Are you getting headaches? Are they frequent? Do you feel the need to experience what you did before again?"

"Absolutely not," Armand snapped, in answer to the last question. "I *have* been getting migraines. They're awful and they won't go away." "Did you *see* anything, though? Other than pain?"

Armand didn't answer, but the look in his eyes did - he'd seen something.

The drug really had accessed his memories, but for some reason, it hadn't touched his better memories. Walter never had a subject that hadn't gotten addicted immediately, let alone getting repulsed and hurt by it.

"Just… go get your bow," Armand grumbled. "Let's get this over with."

Walter reminded himself to look into it further after Armand returned with developments. He told Armand to wait there, and walked around the bus to get his bag.

He froze.

George stood between the two isles of the seats inside the bus. Walter saw him through the window. He was hunched over something. Walter's sports bag was hung over his shoulder, half open. Walter crept closer.

The journal was open, in his hands. Walter had kept it in his jacket pocket at all times, save for this single exception. He'd put it in his bag just a while ago, so that if he needed to intercept Eden or Theresia, he wouldn't have to worry about it falling out. The *only* time he didn't have it with him, and George had found it.

Oh, hell.

Walter's first thought wasn't to panic, but instead, was a road rage of different ideas on how to take George out so he wouldn't reveal a thing to anyone else before they found out. He shut all of those thoughts away and watched George close the journal, and hold up Walter's baggie of pills. Walter crept closer, and rapped his fist against the metal side of the bus. George's head snapped up and around. Walter crouched out of sight. He heard a soft *thunk,* then footsteps as George hurried off the bus.

Walter crept out from the back of the bus. George was at the open hood, as usual. His face was ashen. That nearly would have brought a smile to Walter's face, if he hadn't just been exposed.

George moved closer to the left side of the bus, where Armand stood, away from Walter. Walter took the opportunity to walk as quickly and silently and as normally as he could to the door, then hopped on to the bus and grabbed his bag. It was closed and intact, naturally, for George wouldn't want to be caught snooping. He looked around, squatting on the floor of the pink vehicle, and made sure no one could see him. They couldn't. The only person on the bus was a soundly sleeping Evangeline. She smiled to herself and mumbled something unintelligible, clearly having a good dream.

Walter heard George's voice, talking to Armand. Another voice joined them. Theresia. Walter began to leave, but something else caught his eye.

Armand's messenger bag.

He wanted to leave it behind. But something stopped him from abandoning the bag. It was an odd, stupid compassion, to allow the man he would kill to retain his possessions when he died. Whatever it was, it delayed Walter and forced him to nab the bag, before silently hopping off the bus. He ran to the back of the bus again, and waited to hear footsteps or the sound of George saying goodbye, knowing George would take his place again at the front. The goal was to stay out of the man's sight, and keep a bus's distance between them always. While he kept an ear on the faded conversation, Walter sifted through his bag. Nothing had been taken, he thought. No pages of his journal had been torn out.

Walter took out his Ziploc back of pills. There were three of them, intact. He took out the handkerchief he'd drugged Armand with.

Walter knew to keep it far away from him. The smell clung to the nose and took effect immediately. But there was something new to it that he hadn't smelled before.

Around the handkerchief was the faintest aroma of an old perfume. Perfume, like the one Evangeline wore.

Walter saw her smiling face again—the flashing of her silver cross necklace, blue eyes closed, serene, smiling, dreaming of something good.

A good memory.

Walter's heart stopped beating for a second. The world went still.

He heard George's voice say, "Probably went out to attend nature's call. Tell me when you see him, if you can, I do have some things to discuss. Good talk."

It was almost too loud, as though George wanted him to hear it. Walter listened further, and finally dared to peek out. Theresia walked into the woods worriedly, gesturing for Armand to follow. The moment she disappeared from his sight, Walter raced to Armand, who had started to follow her, and yanked him back. "Come with me."

He pulled Armand away and along the edge of the forest.

"What are you doing now?" Armand hissed. He tried pulling away. Walter couldn't feel a thing. He felt his heart beating wildly, and for some reason, he had not a single thought in his head. He knew what he had to do.

Walter broke into a run, keeping an eye on the back of the bus, but not really caring who saw him anymore. His heart thumping away was the only thing he could hear. He looked back, found no one watching them, and dived into the woods. Armand stumbled behind him.

"What are you *doing*?"

Walter stopped. He swung around, his vision blurry and red and his head spinning and wild, and stuck his face close to Armand's.

"George found the drugs, and I think Evangeline took it. We've been discovered, and we can't stay here anymore. We're getting out of here."

"What?"

"We've been discovered. If we wait any longer, it won't just be Theresia and Eden. The whole lot will be out to get us."

TAMANNA

A new problem had arisen.

Tamanna had just been getting to the good part of the mystery. Evangeline had revealed a part of the mystery of the letter to her, explaining of Nathan Colbert and her identity as a surgeon before retirement, but she hadn't said anything about her name at all, and Tamanna, having gotten distracted, had forgotten to ask further. She'd given her developments to Ilays, who pondered it well, and while they stood silently with each other, just the two of them in a stupid little road with a smoking, dead pink party bus, another party had entered — Armand.

It was clear he wasn't the same as he was before after going out to find the way to the main road with Walter. It was a dumb thing to say, too, because Tamanna knew him for collectively three hours at the max, but she was sure something had happened to him. This was only confirmed when she went back to the bus after talking to Evangeline, who was napping at the time, since her old brain needed periodic resetting. Tamanna figured the chunky phone would have something related to Nathan Colbert, or at least the strange incident of her two names in it. So, she'd nabbed it, only to find Armand sitting right there. He'd been sitting so still and so rapt in his own thoughts that she figured he wouldn't care, or even notice. But he did.

He didn't seem too interested in knowing why Tamanna was stealing a nice old woman's phone. Instead, he'd asked the most peculiar thing: "how long was I asleep?"

When she told him he wasn't asleep at all, he looked at her disbelievingly. He looked like he was having trouble focusing, like he was floating away on a star or something and couldn't be dragged back down to the Earth. But stupid, stupid Tamanna had been so intent on safely taking away Evangeline's phone, that she hadn't even bothered to ask him if he was okay. She slipped off the bus and went to Ilays.

They stood there, pondering about Evangeline's life as a doctor, and just like that, minutes and minutes passed. Before she could finally open Evangeline's phone—to which she knew the password, of course—she felt a tap on her shoulder, and Armand was standing there, looking worse than ever. There were dark circles marring his creamy skin and for a second, it looked like his fingers were trembling.

"Armand, I'm so glad you're here." Tamanna really did feel a rush of relief.

It was a strange sensation, to feel relief and happiness and fear and worry for someone she'd never seen before, someone she'd never seen again, and yet that was exactly what she felt. "Ilays and I have found *so* much and there's so much to tell you-"

"Not now."

"What?"

"I'm sorry. I can't talk to you right now. But I need your help."

The hair on the nape of Tamanna's neck prickled. Something cold bristled down her spine. "What's wrong?"

"I can't tell you right now. For your own safety. But trust me, please.

Everyone on this bus is dangerous."

Tamanna flinched before she could process it. "What do you mean, *dangerous*?"

"I told you, I don't want to tell you anything in case… you know." Armand fumbled and looked back for a second. Tamanna followed his gaze. He was staring at the bus. Or someone in the bus. "I need to borrow your phone."

"My phone?"

"Yeah. But listen to me. I'm going in to… sort of test a theory. I want you to put Ilays's number in your phone—you have your phone with you, right Ilays?—and the moment I send you a missed call-"

"You can't," Tamanna put in. "There's no cell service here at all. This bus sucks."

Armand sighed, a little too hard. "Oh. Right. Do you have good network?"

"Ilays does. I actually don't know if I do."

"Well," Armand said, "If you do, you might get a call from me. If you do, run."

"Run where?" Tamanna couldn't even hear her own voice. Ilays listened carefully, almost suspiciously.

"Away. Remember when Walter and I went to search for the road?"

"Yeah, you said there wasn't one in sight except for this one that we're stuck on."

"That was a lie. Apparently, there's one very close by. Just keep walking straight, that way. If I send you a missed call, start running. Call the police, give them your location, and run. Make sure no one sees you. Promise me. Both of you."

"Apparently?"

Ilays asked, with an incredibly level voice, "What about the others on the bus? Evangeline? She's an old woman. Can we take her with us?"

"I'll leave that up to you," Armand replied. "Apparently?" Tamanna echoed.

Armand refused to meet her eyes for a moment. His jaw shifted - he was clenching it tightly. "Just do as I say. Promise. If it all turns out okay, I'll send you another call."

Tamanna wanted to protest. She wanted to ask. She wanted to be as curious as she needed to be. But through some miracle, she knew not to. She knew that there was something horrible happening, some awful thing that had been unleashed with the omen of the bus breaking down. She knew that for once, she needed to listen, and it made her feel queasy. *What if you don't send me another call?* She wanted to ask. *Where are you going? Why are you so afraid, and why do you care about my safety?*

Who even are you?

All she said was, "I'll wait for your calls. Both of them."

Her hand gave him the phone of its own accord. He took it, and Ilays gave him her number. He nodded and tucked it away. Armand glanced back again, then turned to her with such final determination that Tamanna was sure it would be the last time he looked at her again, and that if she got the first missed call, he'd never see her again, or worse, they would become strangers again.

"Run fast," said he, and then he had walked away.

~ 155 ~

ARMAND

"What do you mean, they've found out?" Armand asked. His feet planted against his own will, and he refused to take another step until he got his answers. This was, of course, an incredibly stupid thing to do, but he found no energy to blame himself for it. His headache had manifested into some sort of an inferno and tore itself through every part of his brain mercilessly. He could hardly think straight. Every time he closed his eyes, he saw the stupid, cursed room, with its flickering light and the cracked sink and the door that he couldn't ever open. He saw his captain's face, and he saw his family. He saw everything he needed except for the most important thing - the damned link between it all.

What these scenes were clicked in his brain only moments earlier - it was his past. He'd never known his past before, and it was normal, and something he was used to. Every time he thought of it, he drew a blank. Just the way it was supposed to be.

Until the drug. The perfect bliss of his amnesia was shattered, and glimpses of his childhood were starting to re-emerge like little curses.

Walter reached over with eyes blazing like black fires, and resumed his iron-like hold on Armand's arm. "Stop messing around. We need to leave, now."

"I'm *done* doing whatever you have planned," Armand growled. "First, I had to risk my life to test Theresia, see if Eden was actually a cannibal, and now I have to run away with you? Why?"

"I told you!" Walter snapped. "George found my stash and I think Evangeline might have gotten it in her. Soon she'll realize what it is, and George is going to have some questions. He could call the cops on me. I'm not sticking around for any of that."

"*I'm* a cop!" Armand hissed. "Could your big, slow brain have thought about *that* before dragging me into all of this? All I wanted was to go see the damn art gallery..." he sighed and dropped the sentence. There wasn't any point. Instead, he crossed his arms, and said firmly, "You're so scared of Evangeline and George finding out about the drug. I want to know what it is. Now."

"Armand, we don't have time-"

"Not anymore." Armand lifted his chin and stared the man straight in the eyes. "I don't care. That thing, whatever the hell that is, it's messing with me. I keep getting these headaches and I keep seeing this stupid dark room and its reminding me of things I don't want to remember. What is it, why do you have it, and why did you use it on me? I want to know and I'm not going anywhere, especially with you, until you tell me."

He stared at Walter. The man towered over him, hulking, massive, and yet Armand looked down on him. For once, he was in power. He had control. His life was in danger, he knew, in so many ways, and yet he finally felt safe.

Walter glared back at him for several moments. Somewhere in the distance, a bird twittered. A branch snapped. A single leaf fell to the ground between them, and disappeared into the grass and the bushes. Finally, Walter looked away.

Armand nearly gasped aloud. He'd won.

Walter glared at the ground for a moment longer, as if he hadn't just hurried into the forest with the intentions of escaping, as if he had all the time in the world. Then his face smoothened. He sighed.

"Armand."

Armand had never heard his name being said so gently. There was something heartbreaking about it. Walter asked, with the most concern a human could possibly have, "What do you see?"

Armand didn't even feel like keeping it from him. Like a faucet had been turned on, he began to spout out details. He told Walter about the room, the locked door, the faces he saw, the names that came to mind - his aunt, his uncle, his captain. He told Walter of his headaches and how they were increasing and how they could get so bad he couldn't see. He stood there, and he told of all his suffering to the man that had made him suffer it. Walter stood silently, absorbing it all, and when Armand finished talking, he worked his jaw and stared through Armand, trying to think of something to say.

A single question came out of him in the end: "Are you okay?"

Armand didn't answer. He didn't know how to. Instead, he asked again, "What drug was it?"

Walter answered, finally. "A hallucinogenic hybrid," he said. "It unlocks your best childhood memories and takes you back to them."

"And that's what makes it addictive," Armand realized. "When the effects wear off, the present seems so dull that you simply have to take more."

"But it didn't work on you," Walter said. Now the coach was looking at him warily. "You said you felt pain. All you saw was…" he shook his head. "Don't you have any childhood memories you loved? What happened to you? A dark room?"

Armand scowled.

"Tell me," Walter implored. "Forget the experiment, forget it all. The drug only takes your best memories, your favorite parts of your childhood, and yet in you… your best childhood memory was you locked in a dark room, all alone?

What happened to you? Tell me. Please." "I can't."

Armand stared at Walter. He felt ridiculously empty, devoid of emotional pain. No, not devoid, only drained.

Walter sighed. "I get it. I'm sorry, I didn't-"

"I can't," Armand scowled. "I actually can't. Psychoactive hypnosis. I had it all erased."

"W…what?"

Armand nearly enjoyed the look on Walter's face. "Yeah. I had it all erased by professionals, just a while after I joined the police academy. My…"

And then it hit him. Captain Romero. "My captain… had the idea of removing…"

He remembered it then - something shifting in a dark alley, a year and a half ago, Armand's gun blazing, smoking, as he shot furiously. Three, four, eight times. Feeling his hands tremble violently through the night. Being called to Romero's office the next day. Being promoted. Talking with him. Crying. The sensation of someone's hand rubbing his back. Then a bright light, straps across his wrists, and the gentle face of a masked doctor. Then darkness. When he'd woken up, three days later, he couldn't remember a thing about the day before. He'd gone to the department and told Romero of this incredible phenomenon. Romero had explained it all to him.

You had a really bad childhood, Armand. Really bad. I don't want to tell you anything else. You're a good cop, and I don't want that to go away. I did it for you, trust me. Just trust me on it.

Trust me on it.

Armand had trusted him. What else could he have done?

Walter's voice pulled him away from the memory - the only memory he had anymore. "I didn't know you could erase your memories like that."

"Most people can't." Armand shifted on his feet, shooing a fly away. "I had the resources, and I guess I was ready to let the memories go."

Walter bit his lip. "After you became a cop, you say? Before you got promoted?"

Armand shook his head. "After. I got promoted…" he smiled bitterly.

Walter's had taken the sandbag of Armand's past and stabbed a hole in it with a knife. "I told you I busted a drug ring, didn't I? That's how I got promoted?"

"Yeah?"

Armand wanted to laugh. "I faked it. It was a setup, the whole thing. They were innocent."

"The people you busted?"

"Yep. They never had any drugs on them. I planted them all." "Why?"

Armand thought for a moment. He tried to think, at least, but his mind went blank. That one hadn't come back. He shrugged. "I don't know. I did, that's all."

Walter stood there silently, like he didn't know what to say. He didn't seem too keen on dragging Armand away anymore.

"Why did you give it to me?" Armand asked, saving the man the silence for guilt. "The drug. I thought it was a threat, to make me spy on Theresia and Eden. You know, because it hurts. But it wasn't supposed to. So why did you give me the drug at all? To get me addicted? Was that the threat?"

Walter shook his head. "I..." he sighed. "Well, the plan was to get you addicted, and give you more if you did what I needed you to do. But then you told me how painful it was, and so I improvised. But the truth is, I also needed another test subject. I needed it. I was desperate."

"Because the rest of them died?"

Walter nodded. "It's so easy to get people addicted to a false reality. If all they can remember is the best part of their childhood, eventually the worse parts fade away. Your childhood innocence and happiness are all that remain. But then, reminding people that the world they live in now is a horrible one compared to the one they think they live in makes them think the worlds are different. In the end, they always prefer the security of their own minds. The human mind is a dangerous, dangerous thing."

"Why were you out there making drugs in the first place?"

Walter shrugged. "I'm a coach. You don't get much money teaching kids how to shoot. I took a loan from a dangerous guy, and promised to get him a profitable drug to slip into the market in return. I had to make him something." "He's still waiting for the result?"

Walter shook his head. "I gave him one of the first versions that I made, the one that I think worked the best. It has its own problems. I'm just waiting for him to figure it out."

Armand didn't have the energy to ask anymore. His headaches had turned into face-aches, and all he could presently focus on was the throbbing on the bridge of his nose. He raised an eyebrow to pose a question to Walter, not knowing himself what the question was supposed to be.

Walter actually answered. "I was on my way to the gym to resign today," he said. "I took this bus, an alternate route, in case they were following me. I was going to leave and pack my bags and skip countries. I mean, I don't think they'll find me here, though."

"So, you..." Armand forgot what he was going to say. He pinched his nose and continued. "Um, so you drugged me in hopes that if he'd find you by the time this is all over..." he waved his hand at the forest around them, "you'd have an actual drug to sell to him - a version that actually works, or whatever."

Walter nodded. He fumbled with himself, and Armand could almost believe that he was only someone in an unfortunate situation, trying desperately to stay afloat.

Almost.

Then he met Armand's gaze. "So, you... you remember things now? It's all come back?"

Armand didn't know how to answer. "It's coming back, probably. It's not all there yet, but it's coming back."

"So, I undid the therapy…" Walter began to talk to himself again. He pulled out his bag, most likely to take out his little journal. He sifted through the contents.

He froze.

Then he looked up at Armand again, and something sinister crackled in his eyes. "So, if your memories are back, the drug *now* will pick the best one, shouldn't it?"

"What-"

He took out a little red pill. Then he stepped forward, towards Armand, as if he had not been running away a moment ago. Armand stumbled back. "Walter, don't you *dare-*"

The world's heart was beating. Walter pounced. Armand tried desperately to shove him away, and yet, as hopeless as he was before, he found fingers being forced into his mouth. A little, hard pill lodged in his throat. Walter held a hand against his mouth again, as Armand tried to spit it out, and as he tried to wriggle away to forsaken freedom, he accidentally swallowed.

He felt the red plastic thing slide down his oesophagus, into his body, for the second time.

"What-" he gasped, stumbling away from Walter. "What have you done?"

Walter had the look of a mad man in his eye. "It should work now," he gasped, awed. "It'll work!"

Armand's stomach turned.

A twig snapped.

The dark room appeared, and then vanished.

Then came footsteps, crunching through the leaves. Armand's heart sank.

They hadn't escaped. They could have, but they hadn't. Armand pulled out Tamanna's phone, searched through the contacts, then called the number under Ilays's name.

The moment he cut the call, Eden's voice appeared from the trees - from no particular place, but as though she was all around them at once, like an omnipresent greater being:

"Hello, boys. Anyone hungry? Because I am!"

"Oh, shoot." Walter slung his gym bag off his shoulder and unzipped it.

Armand realized then, blankly, that he'd brought Armand's bag with him too. He'd really planned a whole escape. There was no time to dwell on the thought, however.

"What are you doing?" Armand hissed. "I'm getting my bow-"

Walter froze.

"What is it?" Armand whispered. "What?"

Walter's face was ashen. "Oh, God. George, he…" "What about George?"

"Twelve arrows. I have twelve arrows. I'm supposed to have thirteen."

GEORGE

George's first instinct was to steal the entire bag. That was, until he saw the pills.

They were bright red, extremely plastic. So much plastic that George could tell it wasn't something someone had to swallow. His next guess was that it was a pill that one had to break open and dissolve in water and drink up. Whatever the case was, it was a drug. And Walter needed it. He literally carried it with him in his bag, possibly to work every morning, considering he was a coach. George knew then, that he couldn't steal the bag itself. It was never a good idea to take an addiction away from an addict. George sifted through the contents, taking note of everything else that there was.

Then he found the journal. There were names and descriptions that sickened George. The pages talked about different people, and what they looked like when they were unconscious, what they felt like to the touch, how their bodies twitched, and from the back, going in, was more writing, this time symptoms and reactions. It was the drug, George knew immediately. But what caught his eye was the last entry.

The name was Armand Ewing. It was far too familiar. George thought for a second. And then it hit him - the police officer. Walter had the cop under his thumb.

George's first reaction was frustration. He'd hoped he could eventually tell the cop about his suspicions of Walter, since that was the easiest way to get the threat disposed of. But he couldn't now. Fortunately, George had another idea.

While pondering all of these racing thoughts, George thought he heard movement. He looked over at the sleeping Evangeline for a moment. It hadn't come from her. It was surely his paranoia that made him panic, and nearly drop the entire bag. George composed himself in the last moment, thinking as fast as he could on his feet. He pulled out a single arrow from Walter's large stash and swiftly tucked it into his pants, hiding it away under his stiff suit. Then he replaced the journal as it was before, making sure nothing was moved, and placed it where he found it. Then he left the bus.

He needed to talk to Walter. If he couldn't snitch to the police officer, he had to take matters into his own hand. He needed to know, at least, what was happening between Armand and Walter, and he had every intention of finding out, until he walked around the front of the bus and found Theresia. She stood with Armand, nervously. The poor girl looked outright terrified —and she was right to. From what George had heard, she'd actually witnessed Eden eating the model's corpse. But for some reason, Armand and Walter seemed to think she was somehow in on it. That idea was entirely ridiculous.

George took a deep breath. He touched his suit once, comforted by the feeling of the hard spine of the arrow, and joined them. Theresia had been muttering something to Armand, and the moment she saw George, she ceased to. Her worried face smoothened a bit, clearly trying to mask her fear. "George, right? Hey."

"Hey. What's going on here?" George asked, casually. His voice remained easy going, but inside he felt incredibly odd. Now that he knew about the two of them, he couldn't stop seeing them differently. He saw the glimmer in Theresia's brown eyes, and he knew those eyes had witnessed something inhuman. He saw the faintest tremor flick through Armand's left ear and wondered if it was the drug taking control. He wondered if all of the names in Walter's book had those tremors.

"We're just talking," Theresia said, far too quickly. Armand nodded.

"I see." George went out on a limb. "Have any of you seen Walter anywhere?"

"I'm not sure, no," replied Theresia, before looking over at Armand. The cop shook his head also, and claimed he didn't know. It was convincing enough.

"He probably went to attend nature's call," George said thoughtfully. "Tell me when you see him, if you can. I have some things to discuss with him. Good talk, then."

"Right." Armand nodded stiffly.

Theresia sniffed. "Speaking of, I do need to go too."

There it was - she then looked at Armand very deliberately, raising her eyebrows just a bit. Armand nodded again, understanding, discreet. George smiled to himself and walked off, back to the front of the bus, where they wouldn't see him. Theresia would take Armand with her, when they thought George was no longer there, and George would secretly follow, ready to pounce on Eden.

Truthfully, he had no idea what he was going to do next, once he did catch a hold of Eden. If she really was a cannibal, he did have to kill her. The way she killed the model. It was only fair. It was justice.

Theresia turned and walked into the forest. Armand followed her, but before he could go too far, Walter emerged from the back of the bus, one of the only cursed blind spots, and grabbed Armand's arm. The man dragged the cop away a distance, and disappeared out of sight. George leaped from his hiding place, almost pulling his arrow out, but they were gone. They were gone, and Theresia was gone. George had hoped they would all converge at some point, so he could confront them all at once. But then again, he wouldn't have enough arrows. Within a split second, a decision was made. George silently followed Theresia. She had a bit of a head start, but he caught up quickly, as she walked deeper into the forest.

The young woman didn't even look back. She didn't seem to realize he was there.

"It's just a little deeper in, mister officer," she said, and George realized that she *did* notice his presence - she had mistaken him for Armand, which she couldn't be blamed for, since he had been following her. It irked him to no end that he could not immediately confront and encounter Walter, but he knew that if what Theresia said was true, then Eden was far more dangerous to him.

They walked deeper into the forest in silence, until Theresia abruptly stopped. "There," she said, pointing.

There was a dark green tarp against the forest floor. Something lumpy lay under it. George's stomach turned. Theresia moved forward, somehow still unable to sense George's presence, and turned over the tarp.

George nearly retched.

Lying half-naked, pale against the green, was Ames. Her eyes were glazed and open. Chunks of her flesh had been torn out near her side, exposing her ribs. A weird smell came from her, not as though she was rotting, but as if herbs had been spread to keep the body fresh longer, or perhaps for flavoring. Theresia stared at it in silence, for a moment, before crouching and pulling something out from the other side.

"Eden isn't here," she said. George could barely hear her.

Theresia continued softly, her back still turned to George. "One wonders how someone can eat a raw human corpse like that." she looked down and touched the object she'd taken from Ames's body. George kept his eyes on her, tearing it away from the carcass. He watched Theresia's slight frame tremble, and her shoulders shift.

Then he heard her say, "It really is all her, I promise. But I told her I'd help.

Incapacitate you, keep you fresh."

Then she swung around to face him. For the first time, she saw herself looking at George, and his massive frame, instead of Armand. Her eyes widened in surprise.

George felt a tear pool in his eye. He was in the midst of nature, the world's gift, and yet he was being suffocated. She *was* in on it. They were right. She knew all along. Those tears, the fear, it was all fake.

If he hadn't gone into shock, he could have defended himself. Instead, he found himself rooted to the spot in absolute horror as the world around him drained of its color. Theresia lunged towards him. A horrible, immediate pain burst in his thigh. He didn't dare look down, but he could imagine blood —bright, red blood against the black and white— spurting across his pants.

George heard himself cry out.

Then the colors all returned at once, rushing away and returning to their former places like the ghastly souls escaping from Pandora's box. George's leg weakened, and he crumpled to the ground, grabbing his thigh.

"What are *you* doing here?" Theresia snapped. "It isn't supposed to be like this, dammit."

She advanced, raising a bloody knife in her hand - the object she'd taken from Ames's body. George watched her blankly for a second, feeling every little drop of blood leave his body. He believed he was going to die, and that upset him.

Then the little, rational voice in his head spoke: *You have an arrow, you idiot. If you can't save it for Eden…*

George stayed still. Theresia crouched before him, touched a finger to her lips, and gazed over his body, trying to determine where she could stab next, to hinder him further. She chose his second leg, and raised the dagger high.

George yanked out the arrow from his belt and lunged forward, ignoring the squeals and sobs coming from the hole in his flesh. He brought the dagger down blindly.

Minutes ticked by. Years screamed past. In a lifetime and a single millisecond, George's arrow buried itself into Theresia's dominant shoulder. Only a second later, like the minute lag between lightning and thunder, Theresia gasped in pain. The dagger fell. George scrambled to pick it up. Theresia's arms flailed, and caught his. She grabbed the dagger's blade, trying to pry it from him. Watching it cut through her skin like butter sickened George, but he had no time to let it sicken him. The two of them wrestled for the dagger. Theresia caught his wrist in the turmoil.

She grabbed his thumb. Then she snapped it.

The digit broke before his own eyes. One second it was wrapped around the hilt of the little silver weapon, and the next, it was hanging around his wrist. His finger burned. He tried moving it, but it wouldn't move.

George didn't feel any pain. All he felt was anger. With his other hand, he grabbed Theresia's neck and squeezed. He let go of the dagger and instead, yanked the arrow out of her shoulder. If Theresia cried out in pain, he didn't hear it.

George stumbled to his feet, pulled Theresia to her feet, and dragged her by her neck to a tree. He pushed her against it, thinking as fast as he could.

"You're a sick, sick animal," he whispered, panting. He looked at the girl, and into her panicked eyes, and wondered how he could ever have called her innocent. She had aided Eden in the killing and consumption of a human being. And she thought herself fit to mother another human? "Where is Eden? Tell me now, and I'll kill you a little less painfully."

Theresia's eyes dimmed. A cold, amused smile spread across her face. In the midst of the pain she felt, she choked out, "Look at you. You're so ready to kill me."

"You deserve it!"

"Ames did too, didn't she?" Theresia asked. George tightened his grip on her throat, and yet she continued. "What's the difference between someone like you, and someone like Eden? You kill people that you think need to be killed. At least she has a use for the body. She feeds a hungry soul."

"She feeds *herself!*" George spat. "How could you eat another human being?"

"How do you eat animals then, hmm?"

"Oh, don't you *dare* pull your vegan stunts on me!" George snapped. "Where is Eden? Tell me now. I mean it, woman."

Theresia laughed, and blood flecked her lips. "Eden's out hunting. Just like you."

It made George sick, when Theresia compared them. He wanted nothing to do with Eden.

"Before you kill me, let me ask you something." Theresia traced his hand with her finger, and flicked his last good thumb. "You're a strong man. This isn't your first time, is it?"

"What are you talking about?"

Theresia's smile grew sinister. "You've killed before. Look at you. You've killed before, just like Eden, just like me, and you have the audacity to call us sick? It takes a special breed of human to be like you."

George felt a tug on his lip. He found himself biting his lip to keep from smiling. He leaned down close, and put his lips next to Theresia's ears.

"I'm a salesman," he murmured. "It's a vicious, vicious industry."

"Let me guess," Theresia said, almost playfully, "You also happened to get promoted to top salesman."

"You're damn right, you are."

George had tried to reason with himself many, many times. But he could never sum what he did as wrong. People who did wrong deserved justice for their sins. And people always did wrong, because they looked out for themselves. And they always had to look out for themselves. George, too, was a sinner. Someday he'd seek the just of judgement himself, and on that day, he would still barter for his benefit. He was only human, but he *was* human.

"So," he asked, feeling his premature victory, knowing Theresia couldn't escape or call for help. "You said you've done something too? What's that?"

Theresia smiled widely, almost proudly. She touched his broken finger, then looked up at him knowingly. George tried to wrap his head around what it could mean. Before he could come to a conclusion, Theresia answered for him.

"The living body is a frail thing, isn't it? Anybody can crush rocks or bend metal or rip a deck of cards. You could squeeze a stress ball and people call it relieving. But when I… well, suddenly I'm the psychopath."

George felt barely any surprise, especially compared to the monumental sickness he'd felt upon realizing what Eden had done. He scoffed. "You look like a weak young girl."

"A blessing, that. No one ever suspects you."

George looked down at her. She had done terrible things, surely, breaking and crushing people's bones, mutilating bodies the way murderers did, only with her hands. But he would have felt the same if she had only stolen some money. She was just a human, who would die, who needed to face her punishment. And George, though certainly unfit, would be the one to administer it.

Theresia seemed to realize that her final moment had come. "Do me a favor, when you kill me, will you?"

"What now?" "Crush me." "W-what?"

"Crush me. The way I do." Theresia looked up at him with soulless eyes. "Tear my skin off; touch my blood. You'll feel good about it."

George thought about it. The ultimate punishment - to kill someone the way they killed others. He met Theresia's gaze, released his hand from her neck, and rammed his arrow through her throat.

Then he turned away. Peace spread through him, as well as the satisfaction of knowing he'd done something right, after so long. He took Theresia's dagger into his hand, and stalked through the trees, searching for Eden, searching for the other souls as damned as his was.

THERESIA

To my dearest children,

Your hair felt so fine between my fingers, bristling and prickling and so dead, uprooted from the foundations that give it life. Your skin, separated from its embrace with muscle, nerve and bone, blanketed my body during the nights and on those cold days - skin over skin to protect me from the howling winds. Inside this shell of secrecy and flesh, I was not helpless. Here, I could laugh. And laugh is what I hoped to do, until my own blood bathed someone's body, my own hair weaving their fabrics, and my own skin ripped from my body, stolen, to shelter them like a womb from the cold. I would forgive them, of course. After all, I know how precious that special warmth, the warmth of someone else, is.

My one truth, my one wish was to experience that. To experience the beauty of sharing a soul in a new, incredible way, to be joined with another person in a way nobody else could ever be. With this, I wish to be special to someone, the way you were special to me. To provide someone the satisfaction of hearing the noises of something as tough as a bone breaking, to provide them with the comfort and happiness that you provided me.

Yet as I sit here and die helplessly, in the very way you did, I feel disappointment. An arrow, of all things, sits through my neck, and blood drips from my throat like the bleeding ruby pendant of the priceless necklace of life and death. My killer walks away freely. He has strong arms, yet he does not break me. He has sound ears, yet he does not listen to my request. My one wish remains unfulfilled. I feel nothing anymore, but disappointment. As I stand here dying, I am disappointed. Even after I am dead, completely and wholly unalive, I shall remain, as some hovering flicker of light in the night sky, and I shall continue to feel disappointment.

I am glad I have saved you from this feeling. I shall see you soon.

Your loving mother,

Theresia Pape.

THIRTY-FIVE YEARS AGO

Bright lights beamed in her face. A single bead of sweat tricked down her temple. Someone moved to her side, and a moment later, a cloth dabbed it away. Her fingers moved of their own accord. Warm metal touched her skin from beyond the gloves. A single itch appeared between two of her ribs, underneath her lab coat. Fifty faces stared at her. The bright light took over, and once it disappeared, Joanna-Marie Blocker was standing triumphantly at the center of the stage, her recovering patient was wheeled away to a second chance of life, and all fifty doctors were applauding to her rhythm.

They dispersed. Joanna waited for them to go, watching talking, appreciating people of the medical field stream through the double doors back to their duties. A single man sat in his seat, a large notepad of sorts in his hand, and watched her carefully as everyone left.

He stood silently, walked down the rows of seats, and held the door open for Joanna as the last members of audience left. Joanna joined him, and together they went to her office.

"If you keep saving people like this, I don't think anyone will be left for us."

His voice was soft and humorous. Joanna smiled.

"Patience, Mr. Colbert. I have one ready for you."

"A fresh one?" Nathan looked at her in surprise. He stood to her right, and from there she could see the little birthmark around the pinna of his left ear. "I thought you didn't have any patients left."

"Some of my operations *were* unsuccessful, after all."

Nathan smiled. The rising doctor had a friend in the mortuary, another one who was a coroner. It was one of the first things that had attracted Joanna to him in the first place. When Nathan Colbert had first written her a letter, commending her talents after a particular session in the operating theater, she'd agreed to meet him out of politeness, and just an ounce of admiration for the respect he showed her.

He'd asked her in a little cafe to be his mentor in the arts. She'd refused immediately. But something about the young man drew her to ask him about himself, and she'd found him to be struggling financially as the supporter of a family of seven. His wife had died of a sudden heart attack after birthing their third child, and along with his children he had to care for his rapidly ageing parents and his two younger siblings. The more time she spent with him, the more she realized that Nathan Colbert was a desperate, lonely man. And she was by no means desperate, but certainly she knew he would be useful to her endeavours.

And then he'd told her of his friends in the more… non alive areas of science. Two of his closest friends worked in not just any mortuary, but the very one that most of the patients Joanna could not save went to. She finally accepted Nathan's request, and took him under her wing under one condition - she would always have access to the mortuary, and the bodies inside, and to all the paperwork and proceedings of each body that had once passed under her own knife. Nathan was unsure of her intentions, but he agreed nonetheless.

Three months later, Nathan went to Joanna's office to ask her of some advice. His friend, a coroner, had told him of some strange occurrences with the bodies arriving to the mortuary, and he wanted to hear his mentor's thoughts on how to act. Joanna was absent, however. He thought about where she could be, and he could only come to the conclusion that she had left to her house early that day. He was about to leave, but he decided first to use the restroom.

The first-floor men's bathroom. It was out of order, like it had always been. Years and years ago, one of the nurses had been murdered in this bathroom by a patient, and ever since, it had been closed. Nathan looked around, and snuck in it. He had no time or patience to walk up a floor and through hallways. Nathan went through his business, and began washing his hands at the sinks opposite to the stalls. He looked up at himself in the mirror and froze.

One of the stalls was barely open. There was no toilet inside. Nathan turned around and opened it further. His heart nearly stopped. Blending into the white of the bathroom wall was a closed door. The outline could barely be seen. Only the ceramic handle jutted out. Nathan put his ear to the door. He heard the faintest shuffle inside. There was someone on the other side. His heart beat so loudly he could not believe it had gone so still moments ago.

Ignoring the intelligence of his mind that screamed for him to stay back, Nathan grasped the handle and pulled it. The door swivelled open noiselessly. Nathan tiptoed inside. He went down a flight of stairs, and into what looked like a basement. It seemed to be completely empty of living people. Only a metal slab and equipment lay to one side. A body lay on the table, half uncovered. Nathan walked to it. "Oh, my god. Milo."

Milo Sanchez, the corpse that was to arrive at the mortuary today. His abdomen was cut open, exposing ribs broken off and organs. Bloody tools lay on the table beside him. Nathan reached out and touched one with the back of his knuckle. It was still warm. Someone had held it mere moments ago.

Then he heard the *click*. Something heavy touched the back of his neck.

"Nathan."

Nathan's heart sank. "Dr. Blocker?"

It was her. The gun left his nape, and he turned around. Joanna stood there, weapon raised, looking far less like the revered doctor he'd hoped to become like. There was something cold and distant in her eyes. "Dr. Blocker," he whispered. "Why did you..."

"I suppose you came here to tell me about the situation at the mortuary," Joanna said calmly. "Let me guess, your good friend, Mister Coroner Chandrashekar, he says that some of the unnamed bodies waiting for cremation have been tampered with."

"Yes..." Nathan's feet wouldn't move. "He says incisions have been made and a lot of them are missing organs..."

He turned around to look once again at the body, and then turned back to her with horror on his face. Joanna never cared too much about the human opinion, but the only touch of regret she remembered feeling was when she saw that look on her friend's face.

"You've been stealing their organs," he whispered. "Why would you-"

"Don't give me that, Nathan, not you. Anyone but you." Joanna glared at him. "You know why."

"You're a surgeon," Nathan mumbled. "But you're paid less than your male counterparts? What does organ harvesting have anything to-"?

"Humans don't deserve money," Joanna said. "Money doesn't discriminate the way they do. I found a fantastic dealer. Money for well-maintained organs. It's more than anyone could dream of making."

Nathan remained silent. Joanna wished he had never discovered her. She watched Nathan warily, her gun still cocked and pointed, until finally, he spoke.

"I won't tell a soul, I promise." "Oh, really?"

"Really. On one condition, however." "And what would that be."

Nathan met her eyes. It was this gaze of his that remained burned in her memory, the last thing that she would remember of him before her disease slowly stole it away, like everything else. Nathan whispered surely, "Make me your partner."

Evangeline remembered smiling, so, so wide.

She was still smiling like that as she blinked, and found herself suddenly in a seat, inside of a pink, broken bus, being shaken to her senses by a young brown girl. Chandrashekar's daughter? *Don't be silly. They're not all related.* Evangeline snapped out of her reverie when she noticed the girl's expression. She looked worried, and from the way she shook Evangeline's shoulder, she was in a hurry.

"What-" Evangeline lost her train of thought. She swallowed, tasting copper. "What is it, deary? Did Mister Driver come back?"

"No." the girl took her arm, gently but firmly, urging her to stand. "We're leaving, ma'am. Now. Please."

"Leaving? Where? Why? Who?" Evangeline's heart was frail enough. She doubted she could handle the excitement.

"The bus. This place. Everything. You, me, and Ilays, the girl I've been hanging around with. We're getting out of here."

"Why? And why on Earth are you in such a hurry?" Evangeline scowled at the teenage girl, but she grabbed her purse and allowed herself to be led off the bus. "Young people, always... where is everyone?"

The girl didn't answer. She took Evangeline's hand as if she was actually the one that was decades older, and led them to the tall Muslim girl standing by. She was the only person there. Both girls murmured to themselves, looking worried.

Evangeline looked around again. The handsome man was gone. The young mother was gone. The punk girl was gone. The young officer was gone. The gym coach was-

He was gone. His bag was gone. His drugs were gone. Evangeline thought about the nap she had taken. She couldn't remember what she had seen in her dreams, but when she woke up, it was as if she never had dementia. Her memory was as it was when she was in her prime. She remembered everything.

From the opening of her handbag, the tip of the book, *Know Your True Worth*, peeked out. Evangeline smiled.

She remembered *everything*.

"Evangeline." The brown girl appeared again in front of her. "Follow us, please. We'll find the main road and get some help. You must be tired of waiting so long." her voice was gentler now. Evangeline raised an eyebrow.

"I'm never in a hurry, dear," she said. She looked over the girl. Brown eyes, but she had glasses. A sharp nose. Good ears. Her breathing sounded stable even though she looked worried. Her arms were nimble, her legs well-muscled. Her nails were trimmed and her wrist bent one way and the other, moving smoothly as she gestured to where they would go-

It's been far too long, darling.

The voice spoke from her own head. It wasn't her that spoke, however. It was Joanna.

"Fine, fine, I'll go with you both, though I have *no* understanding of what's happening," Evangeline said finally. Both girls looked relieved at her response.

They began walking. The two girls murmured with each other. Evangeline cleared her throat, capturing their attention for a moment, and asked, "Could I know your names, first?" she tapped her head. "I keep forgetting.

My apologies."

The brown girl's face smoothened out, as though she was afraid Evangeline's question would be worse. "Tamanna," she said. The Muslim girl added, "Ilays."

"Tamanna, Ilays." Evangeline remembered. She smiled at them, and she continued to smile even after they turned their backs. "Sweet, sweet girls, you two.

Invaluable."

ARMAND

A still ground. A dead wind. Quiet chittering. For one monumental moment, the world held its breath.

And then she appeared.

Her face was as pale as a ghost. Her eyes pure white. Her facade black and white and black against the dark, green forest. Eden grinned, and she became black and white and red.

"Now, now, weren't you supposed to be with me?" she asked. Her finger pointed, accusing Armand.

It took Armand all the effort he could muster to use his head. He exchanged a quick glance with Walter - as quick as possible, as if Eden would hiss and strike if they turned their backs for even half a second.

"So, Theresia was in it, after all," Walter said. His eyes darkened. "I knew it."

Eden splayed her hands. "Guilty. But oh dear, would you look at that?

You're guilty too. Where are you two boys running off to, instead of obediently following Theresia to your death?"

Armand shook his head. "I don't get it. Why would you need to kill someone else? Why would you bait someone and lead them-" Armand thought he finished his sentence, but he never did. His vision darkened, his own voice screamed in pain at him, and when he came to, he finished instead with, "you couldn't have eaten Ames that fast."

Eden raised a thin, black eyebrow. It was drawn on with a pencil. "You're a police officer. I'm sure you know why. Some things are necessity. Some things are just fun. I'm sure you've felt it, too. First you shoot the bad guys because they're bad, and you're good. Then you shoot the bad guys because you like it. And then, you shoot and shoot and shoot because it's the only thing keeping you from locking yourself in your room and quivering from withdrawal. It's the thrill of the chase."

Armand hadn't felt it before. If he did, he couldn't remember it anymore.

Pain dragged itself across his skull, moaning and stabbing at the cracks in his bone, trying to get to his brain. It stabbed along his scalp and around his forehead and temples and finally reached his eye sockets and plunged its way in. Armand shut his eyes. The dark room returned. He was standing in front of the mirror, looking at himself again. This time, he wasn't twelve years old anymore. He was himself in the present, or at least, his reflection was. Whoever it was in that mirror stared at him with hollow eyes, sallow skin, and the most miserable expression one could imagine. Armand stared at himself. He did not move, nor did his reflection. They stared at each other, wearing the same agony and the same dirtied, striped pajamas.

And then a hand appeared next to him, in the mirror. It slowly crept out, taunting, like something of a horror movie, and in a quick second, latched on to his sleeve and pulled him to the side. Armand gasped, and he was back in the forest again, being pulled to the ground. Eden lunged past him furiously and slammed into Walter. The two of them wrestled. Walter was easily stronger than her, and yet, they both were fairly matched. Walter pinned Eden to the forest floor, apparently winning, but Eden reached up, undid her spiked necklace, wrapped it around her fist, and punched him straight in the face. Walter yelled out, more in anger than pain, and backed away from her. The two of them rolled away. Armand watched them heaving - but he didn't know what he was watching anymore. He stood shakily and hit the side of his head with a fist, trying to focus, trying to scare away the pain. When at last enough of it had receded for him to regain his vision, Armand finally saw the scene unfolding before him.

Walter had managed to pull out an arrow from his bag, but somehow, Eden had stolen it from him. Walter scrambled for his fallen gym bag to get another, but as he attempted, Eden flung herself over him, raised the arrow above her, and brought it down.

Armand wanted to move. He couldn't. He watched the arrow sink through the flesh of Walter's forearm, through his muscle and past his bone, and pin his arm to the ground. Walter screamed, and this time, it was in pain. Eden stood slowly, retrieved the gym bag, and produced another arrow. She turned to Armand with a smile.

Her gaze shifted.

Her smiled faded.

From behind Armand came a voice. Deep, charming, and as utterly viscous as the eyes of its owner.

"There you are, Eden. I've been looking for you."

Armand turned around. George stood there, his dark skin melting against the shadows of the trees, his blue eyes piercing like the light at the end of a tunnel. A bloodied knife trembled at his side. Wherever the blade was from, Eden seemed to recognize it. Her eyes widened.

"Theresia-"

"Oh, yes." George laughed humorlessly. He took a step forward, and Armand found himself retreating. Eden stumbled back, too. "I was a fool, this entire time. I thought she was innocent. I thought the lovely, fragile young mother was innocent."

George looked over at Walter, pinned to the ground, bleeding out, then at Eden, who had never looked so scared before, and then at Armand. "You two were right, you know," he said. "I was a fool. Theresia was in on it the entire time. She was working with Eden."

Armand stayed silent. He didn't remember all that he had thought about

Theresia and Eden anymore.

George continued, "See, their plan was simple. Theresia went to you because you were police. You were supposed to follow her into the woods, where Eden was waiting, and once you saw Ames's corpse, once you figured out their plan and realized your mistake, Eden would kill you and Theresia…" he shook his head in disgust. "She'd rip you apart. You were the next victim."

Walter groaned from behind them. "How did you even know about all this?"

George shrugged. "I overheard you two idiots saying Eden was a cannibal.

And she isn't too much of a threat to me, I suppose, but then I realized another truth." he pointed at the fallen Walter. "Your pills. You're experimenting on people. You're drugging him."

And then he pointed at Armand. Now that someone else knew the truth, in the midst of his blinding headache, Armand felt foolish. He was the only police officer, the server of justice, and yet he was the weakest. He'd been used, and he couldn't do anything about it. And now there were dangerous people around him, and his body refused to obey him and call his captain or even the police.

"Now, I don't know that whole story here," George continued his soliloquy, seemingly proud of himself. "But one thing I know here is that Eden needs to die."

Eden's fearful gaze turned into a cool smirk. "Oh? My, my, what are you?

An angel? The punisher of the wretched? Let me guess. Theresia found out it wasn't Armand following her, and you ended up killing her. How else would you have my knife with you?"

George lifted the small, silver blade. "You know what this is?" the question was directed to Walter and Armand. "It's the knife she was using to eat the model's corpse." and then the next question was directed to Eden. "Aren't you afraid, now? It's one against three. Well, one against a much bigger one. Theresia's gone. You've lost."

Eden scoffed. "You think Theresia's death affects me? The girl couldn't do anything anyway. Why do you think she's got that stroller? She couldn't kill a grown adult. In the end, the only thing she was capable of crushing was a stupid rabbit. She was never any real help to me anyway."

George only nodded in disgust. "Typical. I never expected a monster like you to be loyal, even if only to your monster friends."

The air between them was thick and tense. Silence hung only for a single moment, as they all stared at each other, and then, Eden held on to one of Walter's arrows, wrapped her spiked collar around her knuckles, and lunged at George. At the same moment, Armand turned to Walter.

And then he was staring at himself again. The light bulb hanging from the ceiling flickered. His reflection lifted its shirt, and showed off a dark red whip mark on its abdomen. Armand forced himself into the present, head swarming, and hastily ran to Walter's side. He knew what he had to do. Armand yanked the arrow out of Walter's arm.

"What are you doing?" Walter hissed. His voice was low, as if he was afraid George or Eden would stop their fight and attack him if he was any louder. "I'll bleed out even faster now!"

"I know." Armand looked him square in the eyes, but he couldn't really see. Little black and white spots danced across his vision, pulling him not into the dark room but into an empty void of darkness. He wondered if he was already dying. "I know," he repeated thickly. "You have three choices — either you *definitely* die a slow death, or you can either die quickly trying to save yourself or have a chance at surviving. I've chosen for you first. You're not slowly dying with an arrow through your arm. Now you choose whether you're going to live or die."

Walter's expression hardened. He grabbed the arrow that had pierced through his skin from Armand's hands, and unsteadily got to his feet. Armand produced an arrow of his own from Walter's bag, and turned to George and Eden.

George scrambled on all fours, waving his knife wildly in every direction he could reach. Eden danced around him, stabbing lightly through his skin where she could, agitating him, playing with him. Beside Armand, Walter whispered, "I don't know who's on my side right now. But whoever isn't is going to die."

It was a warning, a final warning. George and Eden would die lonely deaths in an empty forest. Armand would get to choose if he would join them. They had spent hours stuck in the pink bus, but now, the final hour had approached.

ILAYS

There's always something different in the air when you know something is about to end. To some people, it feels heavier. To some people, it feels lighter. And to some people, it doesn't exist at all, because they refuse to realize it. If you think about it really, death isn't something you need to refuse. No matter how unnatural the cause, death is a natural thing. Accepting it is one thing, but recognizing it, I believe, should be easy enough. It isn't evil or cowardly to cry for those you love that have been lost. As a person who has lost many family members, I too have cried. But now I realize that these people I have loved and cried for haven't really died at all, as long as their memory remains. When the last person to know them finally forgets, that is when they die. So I ask, in celebrating my funeral, that no one should cry, because contrary to the body of mine present, I am not dead. I will not be dead. Until the last memory of me fades, I shall never stop living.

-Ilays Mehmoud Assaf,

Journalist

TAMANNA

They began to walk in the direction Armand had pointed. Tamanna walked through the midday, two strangers she had never seen before at her side, along a single winding road. Armand's words echoed through her head. There was a thick, clear silence between them. They walked as fast as they could without leaving Evangeline behind. Tamanna clutched her schoolbag tight, imagining it was her lonely little rucksack as she ran away from home. Their footsteps were her music. Her thoughts, Armand's words, were the lyrics. The wind was her melody.

Tamanna stared at the road stretching before, unable to imagine the rest of civilization somewhere in the distance, and suddenly, she felt like crying. She wanted to go home and curl into a little ball somewhere in the safety of her blankets.

Tamanna stood straighter, and quickened her pace.

"Dearie, we've gone quite far," Evangeline said. Her voice cut through the air sharply.

"She's right," Ilays said, glancing back. "We hit a curve or something. The bus is out of sight. I think we're safe."

"Armand said keep following the road. There's apparently a main road somewhere close by. We can't stop till we get there."

"Just for a little bit, dear, if you don't mind." Evangeline said. The strain was evident in her voice, appearing as little wheezes she was clearly trying to hide. Tamanna sighed, and stopped.

"Fine. We can take a little break, just a little one. Like a minute at best."

Evangeline smiled, so dearly, so compassionately. "Thank you. I do need to attend nature's call. I suppose I should just choose a hidden bush or something."

Tamanna almost growled in frustration. She forced herself to calm down, however, knowing old women couldn't really hold anything in. "Fine. Ilays?"

"I kinda need to go too," Ilays confessed. She bounced on her heels impatiently to demonstrate, then smiled in relief when Tamanna gestured for her to go.

"Make it quick, though."

Tamanna watched the two leave. Ilays skipped into the woods as though she was blissfully unaware of the sheer absurdity of the situation. *We are in the middle of a forest, a skip and hop away from society, and somehow, we're in danger and are being forced to run away from the bus we were stuck in for hours because apparently everyone we've been riding it with is dangerous.*

Everyone.

Everyone?

Including the man that had told her this?

Or was he the singular hero sacrificing himself so the three of them could get away?

Was Eden, only a dark humored millennial, dangerous?

Was Walter, the gym coach, rushing to help his students, dangerous?

Was George, the epitome of teamwork and a soothing presence, dangerous? Was Theresia, the sweet, sensitive mother, dangerous?

Tamanna turned to the forest, where Evangeline and Ilays had disappeared into, hesitant. A rustling came, the green parted, and Evangeline returned. She held onto her purse for dear life, as though she was afraid of critters stealing it, and her skirt was rumpled. She smoothened herself out, and joined Tamanna with a smile.

"I still don't understand why exactly we're leaving the bus, darling," she said. "Can't we just wait? Life has never been more still, don't you think?"

"Yeah," Tamanna mumbled. "Where's Ilays?"

"Oh, we'll join her soon. Don't you want to simply wait for the driver?"

"It'll be better if we find the city and get another bus from there."

Tamanna's voice refused to come out louder than a rasp. "Evangeline, where's Ilays? We need to go."

"Oh, don't worry. Young people, always in a hurry." Evangeline shifted her purse to her other shoulder, and edged closer to Tamanna. "Dear, what's your name again?"

"Um, Tamanna."

"Tamanna. Pretty. Tamanna, you know, I like you." Evangeline's wrinkly old hand reached out, and Tamanna found herself flinching. The dotted finger touched the bridge of her nose, and pushed her glasses up. "You have nice hair. Strong grip on your pencil. Well, your eyesight isn't too good, but your brain works well. You walk fast, quickly. In all the time we've been stuck here, you haven't complained about being hungry once. You could have left with that tall friend of yours, but instead you woke me up too. Patient, kind, mentally strong."

A warm breeze tickled Tamanna's arms. She shivered. She felt goosebumps prick her skin, all little fingers, pointing at her and laughing.

"Where's Ilays?" she whispered, but she felt as though she already knew the answer. Tamanna had never understood how a character in a book or a script could be described as feeling dread, and yet the cold, bitter liquid slowly trickling through her joints and down the inside of her skin could only be described as one thing - dread. A painful realisation began to dawn upon her, as Evangeline continued to speak.

"My dear, you still don't understand. She isn't coming." Evangeline smiled, showing off her fragile teeth. "Like you, darling, she has long limbs, and a steady breath and a strong voice. I know how much she's *worth*."

The truth finally became clear to Tamanna with this statement. She had realised what was coming, but when it finally arrived, Tamanna felt like she'd been staked through the heart. It became painful to breath. She knew what Evangeline was saying - worth. Know Your True Worth. Surgeons. Doctors. Organs.

"Oh, I know that look." Evangeline said, almost sympathetically. "That's the look they always have when they know what'll happen next. Do you want to know what'll happen next, what happened to Ilays? All it took was a stone to the head, and there it was - a healthy body with skin like butter."

Tamanna couldn't answer. Evangeline slipped her purse off her shoulder and opened it. Tamanna dared to peak inside.

Makeup. A blocky phone. Papers and papers. Something smooth and shiny.

Slippery.

Bloody.

Tamanna felt herself retch.

It smelled weird. Like the sheep's heart she had to dissect in biology. And it was smooth and shiny and slippery and covered in blood and slippery and bloody and red and pink and rapidly stained the leather of the purse, freshly cut out and-

Tamanna wished she couldn't hear herself scream. She wished she couldn't feel pain when she stumbled back, away from Evangeline, and tripped over her untied shoelace. But she did. The pain shot up her leg like little sparks and traveled through her nerves and muscles and sent tremors through her bones straight into her heart. And it stayed there and clogged her heartbeat and her throat and soon she was sobbing in horror as though her best friend, or her own family had died.

It wasn't the fact that whatever was in that purse belonged to Ilays. It was the fact that it was in Evangeline's purse at all only because Tamanna had insisted Evangeline escape the bus with them.

Everyone on this bus is dangerous. Everyone.

"Oh, enough."

Tamanna only heard it once, but Evangeline, irritated at the common, miserable response, had to say it thrice for Tamanna to register it. "Enough! Shut up. Or what, all the others will hear us and come to *save* you. Isn't that what you want? Miserable…" she composed herself, and the smile returned to her face. It was the same smile she'd smiled at Tamanna when talking of her glorious past, of her dear Nathan Colbert, the same smile she'd appreciated Tamanna with for helping her and talking to her and being a good girl. It was so different, and yet it was the same. "Now, what was I saying? Oh, yes. I like you, Tamanna. That's the only reason you'll know what's coming to you. It's the only reason why this-" she opened the purse again to display, but Tamanna wasn't looking. "-isn't yours, and why you weren't first."

"What about-" Tamanna's voice caught. Her throat felt tighter. She knew she needed to run, far, far away, but for some reason, a reason she didn't know, she wasn't running yet. "What about the rest of her?"

Evangeline rolled her eyes. "Still caught up on the journalist, huh? Dear God, you knew the girl for four hours at *best*. Snap it and worry about yourself, first."

Run. Run. Please, God, let me run. "Why would you want me to worry about myself?" *run, run, run. Now. Run.* "Wouldn't it be more convenient for you if I stayed put? You don't look the type who likes to hunt."

"Clearly you have no regard for personal safety," Evangeline observed. "Bold, courageous… I call it stupid."

Run, run, run, run, run, run- "Or maybe you *are* the type who likes a good hunt and chase. You just don't have it in you. You're getting old, Evangeline."

Rage filled Evangeline's eyes. It was only after the button had been pressed and the emotion fully registered, that Tamanna moved. She watched the elderly woman flare up, determined to rip out another organ after so long, and ran.

TWELVE YEARS AGO

Some people are tough, hardened souls. Others crack easily. A young woman, eighteen years old, found very quickly that she was the latter. It had been four days since she'd been locked in the little windowless wooden cabin, and it could very well be four years until she was let out.

What had really happened was that four days ago, a group of kids, all teenagers like her, had led her into the woods for a supposed camping trip. She had no idea how much they truly hated her. One second, she was hiking along the woods with her best friend, a girl far too similar to her, unfortunately, and the next second, they were both locked in without food or water or sunlight or anything else a human truly required.

The girl remembered the first day they were stuck in there. They'd worked together like they had never done before in school, to try and let themselves out. The door was barred from the outside. Neither of them had the strength to break down the wooden door or walls, and neither of them had the tools required to burn it, if they had even considered it an option. And so, in the end, they'd resorted to screaming and pleading and later yet, when their voices gave out, to praying that someone would come back for them.

No one did. And the truth was not that no one wanted to. The criminals in question, that had decided on this prank to play, later did try multiple times to come back and let the two girls out. The only hindrance was that no one knew where they were. These clever hooligans had stored the wooden prison cell so cleverly in the woods that eventually it became all too clever for them, and by the time their bout of laughing and celebrating was over, they had cleverly forgotten the route. And of course, with the state of mind that they were in, not a single one of them had written the directions down. And so, after three days of searching, they would soon reason with themselves that the cell was not too difficult to escape from, and they abandoned it.

But these clever children were indeed actually clever, to some extent.

Because the prison cell they had locked the two girls in was far too well made for the victims inside to escape from. And so, they were stuck there until someone let them out - and if no one did, then they were stuck there until they died.

Of the two unfortunate victims, the first was calm and rational. She supplied most, if not all the ideas, and when they all failed, stayed calm and optimistic.

This first victim didn't exactly understand what she was doing there, the subject to hate, since she was kind, smart, and somewhat of a pushover. She looked at the girl beside her, the second unfortunate victim, knowing there were some that hated her, and realized why.

In a world of black and white, the colorful ones stand out. And some people don't like that.

The second of the victims, less intelligent and more hateful, knew why she was there immediately, along with her friend.

"You don't get it, do you?" she said, and her friend shook her head. "Look at yourself. Look at yourself and then me."

The friend was silent. The girl groaned, grabbed the girl's face, and hissed,

"The way we look, you don't get it? The makeup and the hair and the ugly rips and scary spikes and-"

"Okay, okay!" the friend was close to tears. "So, we just die here."

The girl nodded. "That's what they want, isn't it? I'm not doing what they want. I'm not dying here."

"Well, what are you going to do? Call somebody for help? No one's here." "I'll survive until someone does come."

"And how do you plan on doing that?" the friend snapped. "Humans can only last a week at most, without food or water. You notice? We have none."

"Shut *up!*" the girl snarled, and they both ended up drifting to sleep, angry.

Their failure to make it out of the cursed wooden shack only tensed their relationship. They screamed at each other and lashed out like dogs chained to a kennel, left to starve. That was what they were - dogs. Mutts. Animals. Scavengers stealing spoils, with nothing to call their own, trying to do nothing else but survive. When the girl went to sleep, hungry, tired, thirsty, and miserable for the fifth time, she realized she couldn't hold on anymore. Not with nothing to hope for and only something to fight with. She was desperate and lonely and angry, but most of all, she was hungry.

Starving.

She turned to her friend, a mirror of misery, and gently touched her hair.

"I'm sorry. For it all. We're both hungry and thirsty and tired. I know." "I'm sorry too," said the friend.

The girl said quietly, "I won't let you starve. I won't let you feel so hurt like this anymore. I can't see you so pathetic."

"What are you going to do about it?" asked the friend, resigning to her fate.

She didn't know her fate had changed.

The girl didn't think. She'd lost the will to, a long time ago. Instead she took her friend's arm, helped her to her feet, and embraced her.

She took her friend's hair in her hands.

And then-

She slammed her friend's head against the wooden walls.

They shook.

A darkening stain appeared on the wood and began to run down, as if the walls themselves were bleeding with betrayal. Again, and again was the first victim destroyed against the wall, rubbed out, torn apart, until her blood became a spring, a pool of water. The girl let the body fall. She saw the corpse before her, and all she could see was red. Meat. Food. Blood. Water.

She knelt like a woman offering herself to the gods. She cupped her hands, took in them some blood, and drank. Then she ate, as she would a large family dinner, and celebrated as she would celebrate a festival. She feasted like an animal. She survived.

And when she had done what needed to be done, she inspected the bloodied walls, and found the force of the death had weakened them. In two hours, she was free. The girl buried the body and began to walk. The silence of the jungle she'd been abandoned in allowed her to mull over her choices, and in truth, she did feel guilty. But she remembered how sweet her friend had tasted, and the satisfaction she had felt - no longer hungry, and no longer captive, and she realized her friend's death would never be in vain. She'd sacrificed herself. She had fed a starved soul. She was a martyr.

A day of walking had transformed the girl. She was smiling brightly when she was finally found by a search party, consisting of her mother and her friend's mother and some of their family. She walked into the light of the human world again, stumbling, grinning, as the desperate group shone their lights upon her, and she basked in their relief. They received her as Sir Lancelot would have received Guinevere. As her friend's mother sobbed, her mother held her tight and cried with relief.

"My darling, darling Eden. You must have been terrified."

"I was, ma."

"You must be so tired, you poor thing, and so hungry. Would you like something to eat?"

Eden licked the blood off her teeth before smiling widely. "I would love something to eat."

WALTER

Walter's phone was ringing. He could feel it vibrating in his pocket as he walked towards a clawing Eden and a struggling George. He knew that it was an unnamed number. He knew the voice on the other end would be slow and raspy. The man speaking on the line would hold his phone in one hand and a ballpoint pen in the other. He would say, *I thought you wouldn't pick up.*

And then, he would say, *I've figured out your little secret. They're all dead now.*

You'll be dead too, but you'll die worse.

Walter pulled the phone out of his pocket. It rang, rang, and stopped. A moment later, it started to ring again. Walter flung it forward. It slammed into Eden's head and knocked her to the ground. George scrambled away, heaving. "Thank you."

Eden screamed in anger, and as George staggered to his feet over her, crawled between his legs, escaping him. She rushed to her feet, latched onto

George's back like a leech, and sank her teeth into his neck. George cried out, arms flailing, and desperately tried to pull her off. Eden tore away from him and turned her head to face Walter. As she pulled her teeth away from George's neck, a chunk of flesh ripped out.

Walter froze.

Eden smiled. Her teeth were red. She chewed.

And she swallowed.

And then, she began to giggle.

George's hand found her arm, and with a yell, he ripped her away and threw her down. Eden scrambled away from him. She wiped her mouth and watched George sink into horror, touching his neck, seeing the blood, feeling the wound she'd made.

"If we all rush at her, we can take her," Walter yelled. He didn't care if she could hear him. She had signed her own death warrant. "George, Armand. We'll take her at once, now."

George gasped out something. Armand didn't respond. Walter dared to look back.

Armand stood just behind him, sagging as if he was a puppet forced to stand on its strings. His eyes rolled over in his head. He whispered something unintelligible, his head rolled to the side, and he drew in a long breath. Then he trembled. His eyes fluttered back, his face pale and sweaty. He shook his head and straightened, then touched the bridge of his nose.

Walter realized, then, that Armand wouldn't be of any help. And that it was Walter's fault, and no one els e's. Walter turned back to Eden.

"There's still two against-"

"Three birds, one stone!" Eden cried gleefully, and threw something at him. It all happened so fast. Walter blinked, and then something sharp hit the side of his head. A stone. It fell at his feet, a part of it bloodied. And then Eden was on top of him. He raised a hand to push her off, and then he felt her teeth sink into his wrist. His fingers went numb. His own blood sprayed across his face. His vision dimmed, and somewhere, he heard George yelling, and Eden laughing. George locked his arms around Eden's waist in attempt to pull her away, but she grabbed his head and slammed it against the ground with surprising strength. George stayed down. Walter's free hand groped the ground. His fingers closed around something cold, and hard. With more disgust than fear or anger, he pushed Eden away, rolled to his knees, and stabbed the stone into her forehead.

Something cracked. The smile on Eden's face disappeared. She threw herself away from Walter, trembling, and touched her forehead. Blood dripped down her face. Eden looked him in the eyes with an expression he couldn't place. She watched him, just like that, both of them heaving, frazzled on the forest floor, for several seconds. The blood leaked slowly down, past her eye, on to her chin. It reached her lips. Eden stuck out her tongue and licked her blood. The smile returned. She raised her hand and slowly wiped her face of the blood. With it went the makeup, smearing onto her hand and showing her skin. It was healthy and pink. Her eyes drifted to George, who lay motionless, the side of his head bloodied.

Eden whimpered a little, then slowly began to drag herself to a motionless

Armand, and the gym bag. Walter growled. "No. No!"

He couldn't hear himself anymore. On all fours, he dragged himself to Eden, ready to kill her off. Eden fumbled with the zips, pulled out something red and small, and pushed it through her lips. Then she took out an arrow and crawled to Armand.

Until that moment, Armand had been on all fours, shivering. When Eden grabbed his collar, the boy woke up. His eyes widened feverishly. He gasped, then snapped out and grabbed her throat with one hand, and stopped her hand holding the arrow with the other. He shoved her away, crawled over her, and punched her in the face. And then again, and again, and again. Then, as she squealed in pain, he took her jaw, and put his hand in her mouth.

Armand let out a quiet sob.

"I hate you. I hate you!"

He took her face in his hands, and ripped her jaw right from her skull. Somehow, her smile remained.

TAMANNA

All Tamanna could hear was her own hard breathing and her desperate sobs as she ran as fast as she possibly could. She was getting tired really fast, but her legs refused to stop. She just needed to go a little bit further, just until they connected with the main roads again. Evangeline wouldn't dare do anything to her in public. She wouldn't do what she had done to Ilays in a secluded part of some forgotten forest-

Stop it. Stop hurting yourself.

Tamanna knew it was her fault for bringing Evangeline along instead of leaving her asleep in the bus. And she knew it wasn't her fault for not knowing what the old woman really was. She couldn't even bring herself to think of the term. *Body thief? Organ harvester. Murderer.*

Tamanna tried to cry a little less loudly as she ran, so that Evangeline wouldn't hear her. She covered her mouth, gasped for breath, and sped up. She didn't even know why she was crying. Evangeline was right; she'd only known Ilays for a few hours, tops. But she had known Evangeline for so much longer.

And she'd never once suspected a thing. She thought of all the times she had crossed the old woman to get to her seat, how many times they'd smiled to each other. Evangeline had called her *dear.*

Tamanna didn't notice where she was going until she hit a crossroad. The roads forked into three smaller roads. She stopped hopelessly and turned.

Evangeline was nowhere to be seen. She was probably wheezing somewhere way behind. Tamanna peered down all three roads, prayed to every god she knew, then dived into the left-most one. She jogged along the path for a considerable amount of time, and just when she was beginning to think she'd have to turn around, she heard it: the sounds of wheels and people. She'd reached civilization again. With a final burst of energy, she ran along the curving road and out of the forest.

There were real life people. Buildings.

Cars.

There were two buildings framing the road she'd gone through on either side. There was a coffee shop in one, to her right, and a restaurant and boutiques to her left. Cars waited impatiently at a signal. On the other side, splitting between the intersections, was another building. Tamanna looked back once again and dove into the restaurant. She found it to be not just a restaurant but a hotel as well. She wished she could sink into one of the rooms, but she had no money.

The truth finally hit her when she entered the lobby. She'd only been stuck in the party bus for a few hours, but it felt like weeks since she'd seen anyone else. Perhaps she looked like a feral child, but she didn't care. She stared shamelessly at the porters and staff and residing guests as if she'd never seen another human before.

A young man in a suit cleared his throat, calling for her attention. Tamanna stared at him blankly. He looked a lot like Armand. "Can I help you, miss?"

Tamanna shrugged helplessly. What was she to tell him at all, that she was being chased by an eighty-year-old organ thief? Who would believe her? "Can I… um, can I have a glass of water?"

The staff's eyebrows twitched with just a hint of annoyance, but he nodded and walked away. Tamanna watched him, then slipped into the ladies' restrooms.

It pained her, for some reason, when she saw herself in the mirror, and found her reflection to be exactly the same as it was in the morning, before she'd gotten on the bus. She washed her face and dried it, feeling feverish, and looked at herself in the mirror. It was still the same. But it was all so different. To everyone but the people on that bus, nothing abnormal had happened. And yet something monumental had begun and ended. Lives had ended. People had disappeared. Ilays was out there on the ground, covered in fallen leaved, a hole in her chest, and no one would ever know.

Tamanna cleaned her glasses, adjusted them on her face, and did her hair up just the way she liked it. When she came out, the staff hadn't returned with her water.

Someone else had, though.

Evangeline stood there, near the entrance, with her hand clutching her purse, and a knowing, mocking little smile on her face. She walked forth briskly, and Tamanna found herself frozen.

"Now, dear," said Evangeline, loud enough for others to hear, "Why did you just leave your poor old grandmother out there like that? Come, let's go home."

She caught Tamanna's wrist and began to pull her. Desperation filled Tamanna, as she helplessly followed Evangeline to the exit. She could not pull away or cause a scene. And she couldn't touch Evangeline. Not with so many people watching.

And then she saw him - the waiter in the suit, holding a glass of water, searching for Tamanna with an expression of resignation. Tamanna's heart leaped wildly, for anything resembling a chance.

With all the courage she had left, she put on an innocent, tired face, and pulled Evangeline towards the waiter. "Excuse me?"

"What on Earth are you-" Evangeline hissed, but she, too, knew she had no

choice but to comply. She stopped Tamanna, and opened her purse just a crack. Tamanna saw flashing silver. She knew what it was. She knew what it did, and it nearly made her heave again. But Tamanna's head was clear enough -or perhaps unclear enough- to disregard the threat instantly and continue to pull Evangeline to the waiter. "Excuse me? Sir?"

The young man turned. Tamanna could see his eyes flicker between them, taking in the new guest blandly. If only he knew. "Hi, sir. Actually, that water wasn't for me. It was for this sweet old lady here."

"Of course, miss," said the man politely, and gave Evangeline the glass. She took it suspiciously, confused. Tamanna only beamed, hoping her lips didn't tremble with worry.

"Drink up, ma'am," she told Evangeline, and took the waiter's elbow gently, leaning in closer, and whispered, "Sir, I need your help."

The man's eyes brightened, longing for adventure. Tamanna wanted to laugh at him. Instead, she remembered what was in that purse, and continued quickly, "I don't actually know this woman. She's been following me for a while, and I think she's convinced she knows me. She's been saying all sorts of stuff, and she even threatened me."

"Threatened?" the man glanced over at a suspicious Evangeline. "Yeah. I think she has a knife in her purse."

The man's lips formed an 'oh'. He murmured, "Would you like me to inform the authorities?"

He was no longer a waiter. Now, he was a hero without a cape, ready for action.

Tamanna shrugged helplessly. "I mean, I don't know if it's actually a knife,

and I'm sure she's a harmless old thing. I mean, no offense or anything, but look at her. She's just been nagging me a lot, so maybe if you could call the hotel security, just make sure that isn't a knife, and send her off or something…?"

The man nodded. "Absolutely." he straightened and walked over to Evangeline. He put his hand on her back and bent over a little to reach her ears, and spoke to her calmingly. Whatever he said enraged Evangeline. She pushed him away and glared at Tamanna.

"You little-!" she gasped. "I should have killed you when-"

"Ma'am, I apologize," said the waiter, "but you can't go around threatening others. I'm afraid I'll have to have hotel security escort you away."

"You don't understand, she-"

"Ma'am? Do you know which retirement home you belong to?" he asked, and gently yet firmly, led her away.

It was over. It was all over.

Tamanna thanked the waiter once he returned, then fled back to the restrooms, locked herself in a stall, and quietly cried.

WALTER

Walter always told his students one thing:

"Curiosity kills the cat. But never forget, satisfaction brings it back. So always question. Not just what you think is wrong or unfair, but what you think is right, too. Always question."

He encouraged his students to be curious. To ask what made someone worthy of going to the finals of a competition, and what made them unworthy. To ask what would happen if they broke a rule, or what would happen if they followed it. To ask what happened when you string a bow the wrong way or accidentally broke something valuable, because only if you knew would you decide what to avoid and what to embrace. Naturally, with all this talk of finding answers, Walter had become a curious man. And he would be an idiot if he didn't think of what would happen if he took a loan from a dangerous person. The curiosity remained in him far after he'd submitted a doable drug - what would happen if he made a better one? What would happen once they finally caught up to him?

And now, he'd been presented with more questions? What had Theresia really done? Why had George been so hell-bent on killing the two women? Had George done something too? What had Armand forcefully forgotten? He so desperately needed to know.

Curiosity kills the cat, and satisfaction brings it back.

But the thing is, most people don't realize - curiosity *kills* the cat. Satisfaction simply can't bring it back. Because the cat has already been killed. It's over. The cat is dead. With curiosity, is where it all ends. The story is over.

ARMAND

$\mathbf{I}$t would take her a few minutes to die.

Armand had to keep his jaw clenched tight to prevent the headache from building. He stood, feeling weaker than ever. His vision darkened and reddened and pulsed. An entire showdown. A huge fight. And what had he been doing?

Crying in a little room like a little boy, begging his uncle to let him out. *I've been good today, right?*

Armand took out Tamanna's phone and dialed a familiar number. He put the phone to his ear, hearing it ring. The sound was oddly soothing.

From under him, Eden twitched. The blood on her neck gurgled, as if she was trying to speak. Armand felt his police instincts flare. He dropped to a knee, pried the arrow from her dying hand, and stabbed her through the heart twice. He wished he had his gun. The call went through, and a voice said, "Hello?"

The voice on the other end of the line belonged to Dwight Romero.

"Captain." Armand wanted to cry.

"Armand? Where are you calling from, son?"

"About that, sir. There's been a situation." Armand proceeded to quietly explain what he could. He told his captain of the cannibal and her demise, of Theresia, Ames, and the hopefully safe Tamanna; Evangeline and Ilays. He asked Walter the name of the man he'd borrowed money from, as well. Romero listened patiently. Armand concluded by whispering, "I'm speaking from Tamanna's phone."

He found himself blacking out again. This time, it was far simpler. There were no rooms and no mirrors and no flickering lights. Instead, he found himself at a cafeteria, eating ice cream with his captain. The man, like a father to Armand, was speaking gently.

"It'll be okay, son. You can trust me on that."

Armand, who remembered nothing of his entire life before, smiled happily.

"Okay."

"Can you hear me?"

Armand sighed, and he was back in the forest with bodies around him. He felt his heart thump dully in his chest, reminding him with annoyance of how he was still alive. "Sir?"

"Are you okay?" Romero asked. "Yes sir."

"Ewing." the voice was a warning. Armand knew he'd said something, probably something stupid while he'd faded out a moment ago. He sighed louder. "Sir, there have been some complications. I'll tell you about it when you send your men here. I need to assure my safety, and the safety of those that are still alive."

Romero would know something happened. He didn't press the matter. Instead, he said, "I'm sending men immediately. What's the crime scene like, where you are?"

Armand looked around. He caught Walter staring at him, wide eyed. Next to him was a motionless George. Armand went over, knelt over the man, and checked his pulse and breathing. "Two bodies where I am and there should be two more bodies close by. One man and one woman here, and two women over there. One conscious witness."

"Stay with them, Armand. I'm coming."

"I can't, sir. I need to find the other three and make sure they're safe too. I don't think there'll be a problem if I leave the scene."

"Only if you have to." Romero sounded displeased. He had the right to be.

Armand was a terrible cop. He ended the call and pocketed the phone.

Walter swallowed dryly. "So, you said four bodies, huh?"

Armand nodded. He couldn't look Walter in the eye anymore, and he wasn't sure if it was because of how useless he'd been, or because of what an awful person Walter was.

Walter continued. "That's, uh, Ames and Theresia there, the two women, and here, Eden and George, right?"

Armand retrieved his messenger bag, which had fallen astray during the fight. He pulled out his soiled clothes, the one with Gatorade stains on them, and packed his jacket under George's head. "Actually, George is alive. Might have a concussion, definite trauma to the brain and skull. But he'll live."

"But you said there were two bodies here, a woman and a man-"

Armand's vision faded again. This time, he was not himself, but a large, burly prison inmate wearing orange and a sleeve of tattoos. He walked across the little cell, watching his cellmate squirm away in fear. It was a small man with tanned, weathered skin, and calloused hands from using his belt as a whip. Armand backed his cellmate into a corner, then pulled out a sharpened spoon and knelt over him. He plunged the shiv into the man's cheek, then through his other cheek, then through his nose and mouth and neck and his raised hands and his chest and stomach and his gut and liver and intestines and then through his lungs and his heart. He stabbed again and again and again and again and again. When he knew the cellmate wouldn't fight back, or move at all ever again, Armand, the large criminal leaned over and whispered:

"Your nephew, he says *hi*."

When Armand returned to his own body, he was holding a shiv - except the shiv was in fact a large, sharp, blood-stained rock, and the large man was actually his cellmate, and his uncle's stabbed body was actually Walter's bludgeoned body, that would have turned to mush if it had been bludgeoned just a bit more.

Armand stood.

He drew in a long breath.

Then he turned, picked his way out of the forest, and broke into a run, to find some people he had met only hours ago - the people that mattered most. He ran away from the bodies and the blood and the drugs, and he ran away from the pink bus.

***

Somewhere in an alleyway, a man smiled morosely. He'd always told the people that looked at him like he was a looney, that he was Kharon. No one ever understood, but it didn't really matter to him, since he did. In Greek mythology, Kharon was the charioteer of a deathly steed, a boat that crossed a river into the underworld. Kharon carried the dying to their deaths. He brought them from the land of the living to the land of his death. That was his duty. Not many thought of him immediately when thinking of Greek mythology, and yet, he carried a burden as large as any other deity's. Many must have overlooked him, saying he was just another hollowed spirit working for Hades, the god of the underworld, but there was a truth the man knew that Kharon knew: most of the people that were carried upon that boat to their death weren't simply destined to die. They were already dead.

The man raised an unlit cigarette, then looked at it, and put it back in the case. He was trying to quit.

TAMANNA

The waiter returned a hero. The man found Tamanna sitting at one of the tables outside, drinking water. He asked her if she wanted anything, gently. She shook her head, because she had no money, but he brought out for her a cup of coffee anyway, on the house. He then took time off his shift to sit across from her and quietly deliver the news.

"That old woman that was following you," he said, "It's a good thing we got the security. She did have a real knife, after all."

Tamanna waited.

"They found something else, too," he continued, uncomfortable. His voice dropped. "They thought it might be, well, an organ of some sort. Still fresh."

Tamanna knew it was to come. She had counted on it. She still found herself gasping and covering her mouth. She heard herself controlling her tears, and it was pathetic. The man patted her shoulder awkwardly. "We've already called the police. They came in and took her away, just like that. So, you dodged a bullet, there."

Tamanna nodded, and thanked him for the help. He carried on, telling her how Evangeline had been questioned by the security while the police were still on the way, how she had continued the ruse of being a forgetful elderly lady, pretending to have amnesia. She had been taken away moments ago.

Tamanna thanked him again and again. It was all she seemed capable of saying anymore. He asked her if she needed to be taken to the police as well. She politely refused, and thanked him for the coffee. He nodded then, finally, and left. She would never see him again.

TWENTY-FIVE YEARS AGO

The Doctor's Club, was what they called it informally. It consisted of only two people. No one else knew it existed. The Doctor's Club had its own special password and treehouse, but the password was only the faces of the two members, and the treehouse was a little summer cabin in the woods.

In the cabin, on that one particular day, sat the two doctors of the club.

Joanna-Marie, the founder of the club, watched her protege fondly as he brought them some snacks and a magazine.

"Your own book, huh?" he said with a chuckle. "I can't even believe it."

Joanna smiled. "I wish this could last forever, you know. I know it can't and its stupid."

Nathan shrugged. "Of course, it'll last forever. It'll last as a memory to me.

I'll never forget this."

"Me neither," Joanna said warmly, and they clinked their glasses of guava juice to it - *to never, ever forgetting The Doctor's Club!*

"When we eventually retire, you know, because of course we will someday," Joanna said, "What do we do?"

"What do you mean?"

"When we leave all of this behind, we have to *leave* it. Forever. No one can know."

Nathan's eyes dimmed in understanding. "Um, we can change our names.

Fake identities. I'll say we've summed up enough to do that."

"Fair enough." the idea was ridiculous. So ridiculous that the mature Dr Joanna giggled at it. "What will you name yourself?"

"I don't know!" Nathan grinned. "What, say, Nicholas Apollo?"

"Ooooh, Mister Nicholas *Apollo*," Joanna teased, squealing with childish laughter. "I like it, I like it."

Nathan shook his head with a stupid smile and raised his glass. "The very and the same, Mister Apollo speaking. What about you?"

Joanna thought very seriously for a moment. She shrugged. "Maybe something biblical?"

"Biblical?" Nathan wrinkled his nose. He'd never believed in the same things as her. "Why?"

Joanna spread her arms around her. "Look at us!" she cried. "We're the working hands of God!"

Nathan burst into laughter, and Joanna laughed with him, obnoxiously. "No, really! Something pretty, like Eve, or Evangeline. Doesn't that sound nice?"

"Not really." Nathan swirled his juice. He shifted a little. They were both sitting cross-legged on the floor. Nathan liked sitting cross-legged like that, but he had developed a sort of leg pain that prevented him from doing so for too long. "So, if we somehow forget-"

"Which we won't," Joanna said sternly.

"But *if* we do," Nathan spoke over her, gently. "Somehow. I don't know, just somehow. We'll promise to remind each other?"

"Why would we do that?"

"So, we can keep in contact, and help each other out. Promise."

"Yes, yes. I promise." Joanne waved it off. "No, but really, on the topic of promises, will you promise me something?" "What?" Nathan became serious.

Joanna held up her pinkie. "Let's promise each other, to never, ever get caught."

"How would we get caught if we faked our identities and-" "Shhhh. Just promise me."

"Fine. I promise." Nathan's eyes twinkled. "If I get caught, you're taking me to the grave."

"Yes I am." Joanna rolled her eyes. He could never stay serious. "I promise to kill you if you get caught, you idiot."

Nathan beamed. "And my dearest doctor, I promise to do the same."

ARMAND

The twelve-year-old boy could finally open the door. When he did, he was in the sky, and the clouds were made of cotton candy. He jumped from the door to the closest cloud, but when he set foot on it, his feet burned, and so he ran across the first cloud to the second. The second one felt like a hot tar road. He turned around to return to his room, but instead, he found himself in the forest, right where he started, before Ames's chewed corpse. Her face had been eaten off and replaced by Eden's dismembered jaw. Armand turned away from it, and rammed headfirst into a thick, blocky tree. But it wasn't a blocky tree; it was Walter's chest. The gym coach, still full of bloodied holes, grabbed the back of Armand's head, and pressed a cloth over his mouth again. And then the sharp crystal of pain began to form beside him again. Before it could manifest fully, Armand struggled to lift his arm. He took a sharp, painful shard, and ran Walter through with it.

Then the phone began to ring. It wasn't his ringtone, a painfully generic default, but instead, some old, charming Bollywood classic. He had no idea how he knew what it was. He'd never heard a Bollywood song before. Armand opened his palm, and the phone fell into it. It had a glass case and hurt him when he held it.

The glass cut into his palm and the pain shot up like firecrackers along his arm and into his eyeballs. Armand picked up the call.

"Uncle?"

TAMANNA

The voice on the other end was Armand's. For some reason, Tamanna had been so afraid that it would be someone else's.

"It's me, Armand. It's me, Tamanna. Are you okay?" Armand was silent. Then his voice crackled quietly. "T-Tammana?"

Tamanna nearly cried again, for a reason she didn't know. Why did his voice sound so broken? "Yeah, it's me. You won't believe what happened here. Are you okay?"

"Yeah."

"Where's everyone else? Should I call the police."

"The… police?" It was like he'd never heard the term before. Then his voice   became stronger. "Uh, no. No. I got it covered."

"Okay. Come here as quick as you can. Follow that road, you know, where you pointed to, and when you reach a fork, take the road to the very left." "The… uh, what?"

"The left most road, Armand. Take the road to the very left!"

"The, um, okay." Armand said, sounding almost delirious. "Stay safe."

"Armand! Where's everyone else? What happened? You said everyone was dangerous and…"

"Oh, they're dead." this time, his voice didn't sound disconnected, or unfocused. It was sharp and cold and utterly unsympathetic. It was the only thing he was sure of. "I'll be there. Road to the very left."

"Yes. God, I have so much to tell you. Come fast."

And then she cut the call. Her heart sank, like a warning. She had a feeling it wouldn't be over until Armand was sitting in front of her, and they could both clear things out.

The sun reached the very center of the sky. Tamanna looked up at it, squinting. It was warm outside, but she was shivering.

ARMAND

The boy finally found his way back to the dark room. Armand slipped the phone into his pocket and ran with renewed energy, and at the same time, he was the young boy, running across the clouds. With what consciousness he had left, Armand held his hand up to his neck. He was burning up. He had no idea what Walter had changed in that drug, but he knew at once that this version was perhaps the most degenerative.

Armand thought he was dying. It made him sad.

He reached the fork Tamanna had warned him about, and somehow, against all the odds, he remembered which side to take. He dove headfirst into the one to the left. His feet burned in his dress shoes, as if he was running on the road barefoot in summer. He felt his face flush, with sweat and fever. Still, he ran. He ran until he heard sounds, and until the forest cleared way into an intersection, with regular non-pink cars and regular non-murdering people. He looked up ahead the blinding sun, and then white engulfed him.

He was back in the dark room. The cursed, dark room. This time he was shaking uncontrollably, and laughing like a madman. Armand spun in circles around the little room, ecstatic. He had no idea if he was still running in real life. He didn't care. When the sun hit his eyes, he felt a tremendous burden lift from his shoulders. If he was still outside, on the clouds, he would have flown. Armand danced around, then finally stopped, panting, and looked at himself in the mirror.

He looked like himself again. He was strong and healthy and smiling. He wore a police uniform and a badge and a cap and a belt. His name gleamed on the badge. He saluted to himself, laughing in amazement. "Officer Armand Ewing, reporting for duty!"

He laughed with so much force that the mirror cracked. It split in the center and drew webs outward. He stared at the crack in amazement. The walls were moldy and the lightbulb was frazzled and the bed had three loose springs, but the mirror had always been perfect. And now it was cracked. Armand's reflection distorted, but his smile never wavered.

"It's happening," he told himself. His fever spread from his face to his body, flushing his skin and turning him pink. His fingertips were numb. "It's actually happening! I've done it!"

A bright light seeped in from the cracks. It framed the mirror and his reflection, and turned brighter and brighter and brighter. The cracks grew. "I've finally done it!" Armand yelled in joy, and he threw his hands up into the air. The mirror screamed and shattered into a million pieces, and the light burst out, unrestrained, and enveloped the universe around him. Armand laughed out with joy, as the glass shards sliced through him,

"I've done it! I've finally broken!"

TAMANNA

She never saw him coming out. Tamanna zoned out and stared at a little ant on the table, hugging her coffee mug, mulling over everything that had happened. When she came to again, people all around her were running away to the road.

Tamanna straightened, coming to her senses, and stood.

That was when she saw it.

A crowd had formed in the middle of the road. A silver sedan had swerved and stopped abruptly in the middle of the intersection, causing a jam. Drivers came out to see the commotion, and joined the crowd.

Tamanna had never felt so much dread. She broke into a run, pushing her way past people, and got to the center of the crowd.

In the middle of the road lay a body. The body lay peacefully in blood. Closed eyes, limp limbs. An ill-fitting tracksuit stained red. Tamanna's broken phone.

There was a smile on Armand's face, even as the life drained away.

ARMAND

A dark, empty void. The surface beneath him was invisible, cold and smooth. A slight shiver ran up his spine. In the middle of the abyss was a shining glass crystal. It pulsed gently. It glowed white. He heard muted smiling and laughing.

When he took a step forward, it was as though he was wading through water at the beach. Something cold tickled his ankle, and droplets flecked his chest.

Then he looked down at himself. He was barefoot, and almost completely naked. He was wrapped in a toga, only a single, cleverly arranged silken cloth, like a Roman God. He caressed the cloth, smiling, and snuggled against it. He was safe.

He looked up then, smiling still, and walked to the glass crystal. It didn't pain as it did before. There was a slight sting behind his eyes as he advanced, but it quickly disappeared, and all he was left with was empty happiness. He was dead, he knew. It no longer made him sad.

He reached out with a trembling finger, and touched the crystal. It reached out to him with hands of carved glass, and held him. It spoke to him of a heaven with yawning green hills, yellow poppies, and a dark cobblestone road with rolling white bicycles. It whispered to him, assuring, that his brain was no longer rotting away, tearing open hidden folds to unleash painful secrets and forgotten memories. Here, it told him, he was free. Then it showed him the heaven, laid him on the green grass, tucked a poppy into his hair, and gifted him a white bicycle, and left him to be. He found himself so immensely happy that he couldn't help but weep with joy. But by the time the beautiful glass figure left him to his own devices, he was tired and inane. The moment the thing's prying eyes left him, he began to search for a way out.

Armand looked upwards, to the heaven of the heaven, and screamed, "Let me out!"

TAMANNA

It was evening when Tamanna found herself in a metal chair in the hospital. Her phone had not been returned to her yet, taken as a part of police investigation. She knew her father had probably called multiple times, sick with worry. Tamanna didn't know what and how to explain the entire incident to her parents that didn't let her stay with her friends past nine-thirty in the night. They would never let her go on a public bus again. They would force her to abandon her emo friends. She would never be allowed to interact with adults again. She'd be homeschooled.

Tamanna made up her mind, then, to beg whoever was in charge of the investigation to keep it under wraps, or at least omit any mention of Tamanna from it in the newspapers.

As if the gods were listening, a shadow crossed Tamanna's view. She looked up. A man stood before her. He wore a white and navy uniform with a cap and a shirt adorned with metal badges and ribbons. Clearly an officer of distinction, like a captain or something of the sort. He looked down at her with sharp eyes.

"Tamanna… Raghavan?" *Australian descent.* She had no idea how she knew, but she did. She nodded.

The man nodded back. "I'd like to have a talk, please. My name is Dwight Romero, and I'm in charge of the investigation of the incidents of the pink public bus."

****

There was a cafe on the other side of the street, opposite the back of the hospital's main entrances. Captain Dwight Romero started by ordering two decafs, the type of coffee Tamanna had only ever heard of in first-person bildungsromans. The man then pulled out a giant wad of a file, opened it, and began to recite a story. It was the story of a pink bus.

"Are you aware of Armand Ewing's condition right now?" the man asked.

Tamanna fiddled.

"He was hit by a car?" she guessed. "But he seemed kind of jittery before that too. I called him, and over the phone he spaced out for a second and called me his uncle or something. But he pretended like it didn't happen a moment later, so I did too."

"Well, yes." Romero nodded. "The doctors found something else, in his system. A drug type we haven't encountered before. It pulls your best childhood memories and attaches you to them, and once the effects wear off, real life seems unbearably miserable, addicting you to it."

Tamanna took in the information silently.

"I don't know if it's my place to say this, but Armand had a bad upbringing," Romero said. "His mother died in childbirth, leaving his underqualified father to work for them both. Ewing Senior couldn't support his family, so he gave Armand to his brother's family. Armand stayed with them and his father visited every day. When he was eleven, his father committed suicide, and his aunt and uncle became his legal guardians. Turns out they were abusive. Eventually Armand joined the police taskforce, and I found out about all of it. I introduced him to psycho hypnosis, and had his memories erased. The drug brought out—"

"So…the drug got confused when it didn't find anything in his head, and brought out everything? That's why he called me uncle?"

"Precisely. That brings us to this man." Romero took out a little passport sized picture. Tamanna recognized him immediately. "Walter Lynch, a gym coach. He was the man giving Armand the drugs. He'd taken a loan from someone dangerous, and promised a new drug, somehow, in return. He spent most of his time trying new variants, but all of them seemed to have major problems. In the case of Armand's variant… well, you know. It couldn't find his memories. It messed with the brain and rotted it. Armand was already dying before he hit the car."

"Oh."

Tamanna felt far sadder than she should have. "So, you've arrested Walter?

Armand did call you, didn't he?" she remembered him saying he had it under control, right before he'd been run over.

Romero nodded. "He did. My men found Lynch's body. He's dead.

Bludgeoned by a rock, died of blood loss."

Tamanna blinked. "How-"

Romero shrugged. "I don't know. But twenty-six punctures in his body, seven bones cracked, and two litres of blood loss says something about the person that killed him, hmm?"

Then he laid out two more pictures - Eden and George's. "These two were the others found in the crime scene Armand reported. Eden Lim and George Torres, left and right pictures respectively. You know any of them personally?"

Tamanna shook her head, and he continued. "From what Armand said he witnessed, Eden Lim is a cannibal."

"W-what?"

"Her DNA has been found all over a half-eaten corpse belonging to a woman named Ames Perrault. She was one of the travelers on the bus you were on." he pulled another picture out.

"I know." Tamanna remembered the model's red hair and polished appearance, and felt sick. "A *cannibal?* She ate people?"

"Many others besides Perrault. We're currently tracing back a list of some of her other victims, and we think her cannibalism may have begun as early as when she was a teenager."

"Oh, my God."

"Now, Armand said she was working hand in hand with this woman, another traveler on the bus, Theresia Pape. This woman has been found by my officers to have killed several children and some animals with her bare hands."

"Oh, my God!"

"My men have also found her dead. She was stabbed through the jugular by who we believe is George Torres, based on the DNA evidence provided by the scene. Now, Torres, Lynch, Lim, and Armand seemed to have some sort of scuffle a few yards away from Perrault's body, and in this scuffle Eden Lim and Walter

Lynch died. We're not quite sure who killed who yet, but the bodies are all in bad shape there."

Tamanna croaked, "What about George?"

"He suffered a concussion, trauma and bloodloss, but he'll live. We did some research on him when we found his DNA on Theresia Pape's murder weapon, and we found that he's killed before, as well. Torres was directly involved in the death of his colleague, and his motives seem to be competition."

"Oh, my God." Tamanna nearly sobbed. She thought of how she'd sat in the same bus as them only hours ago, and she nearly cried.

"Is this all too much-"

"No." Tamanna cleared her throat and looked him in the eye. "N-no. Keep going. What about the rest of them?" she wanted to hear about Evangeline.

"Well, you might be wondering at this point how you got into this situation at all," Romero said. "Your bus abruptly breaks down in a secluded area, none of you seem to be able to catch any sort of signal, and murderers are revealed when your bus driver doesn't return for a long time. Did you think this was-"?

"Suspicious. Yes." Tamanna straightened.

"Well, then, you were right." Romero placed another square photo down. It was a man she'd only seen and noticed once before - the driver. "Gared Mandela. He's the mastermind behind this showdown. He was seeking personal revenge against one of the people on the bus. Remember how I said George Torres killed his colleague?"

It hit Tamanna. "He was related to the victim."

Romero nodded, looking almost impressed. "Mandela's brother, Jeoff Mandela, was a salesman. He carried top position in his division before mysteriously committing suicide. Gared was seeking revenge on George. We found portable signal jammers in the dashboard, and evidence that one of the tires was tampered with beforehand. The whole thing was premeditated. Gared left a whole stack of evidence for someone to find. Pictures, news clippings, letters, printed out screenshots of texts, evidence that George Torres had — at least planned to kill Jeoff Mandela."

"So, he knew about Eden and Theresia and the whole lot of-
" *murderers.* The word stuck in Tamanna's throat.

Romero shook his head. "He didn't. That, actually, was pure coincidence.

But you're partially right. Mandela knew there was a murderer, a clever killer who would definitely find the truth out, given time and clues. He was hoping this killer would get revenge on Torres if he left the bus on its own. This person would find the proof that Torres needed to die, and do the deed for Mandela. Unfortunately, because of, well, everything else, the evidence he'd hidden on the bus was never found by anyone on it at all, and revenge was gone unadministered."

"Who is it?" Tamanna asked, but she didn't want to know. "Who needed to find the evidence and take revenge?"

Romero placed down a final picture.

"Ilays Mehmoud Assaf, a prominent journalist on the human emotion and conscious. We wouldn't ever have known if we hadn't caught and interrogated Gared just half an hour ago. As it turns out, Ilays had been sent multiple complaints from rising actors of a certain acting school, about a director that was exploiting his students. She got the complaint, and somehow, three weeks later, the man died of an overdose. We haven't found her directly linked to his apparent suicide, but we're looking into it at a deeper level than did the officers on scene."

Tamanna found herself stammering, "But she isn't a murderer. She did the right thing, didn't she? She's a hero."

Romero offered a one-sided shrug. "I suppose. Like I said, we're looking into the matter right now, but we can't seem to find Miss Assaf anywhere. She *was* on the bus, we know."

"She's dead," Tamanna said flatly. Something empty thumped in her chest.

She felt shallow. Romero raised an eyebrow.

"How do you know?"

And then it was Tamanna's turn. Instead of telling him everything she knew about Evangeline, she ran a hand over her face and said, "Can I come in and give you guys an official statement sometime this week?"

Romero nodded sympathetically. "Tamanna." Her name had been mutilated by his accent, but still, she listened. "You might be wondering why I've told you all of this."

Tamanna hadn't even once wondered it. She deserved it.

"Of course, in part, it's because we're releasing this very statement soon, and you're the only living, conscious witness," confessed Romero. "And I also think you deserve it."

"But that isn't it, is it?" "No."

"Why are you telling me all of this, then?" "Armand told me to."

Tamanna's voice stuck in her throat. She looked into the man's eyes and saw a soul.

"He called me to report the crime scene," said Romero, a little wistfully.

"The same way he did for you, he blanked out between our conversation and called me *uncle.* He said a lot of things I couldn't understand, but then he told me to find you, the owner of the phone he was using, and tell you all of this. So here it is: the raw truth as we've found it. I'll keep you updated as the investigations go on, as long as you can cooperate and tell me your side of it."

Tamanna stayed quiet. She was afraid of how her voice would sound if she dared to speak. She looked at the coffee mug in front of her, the patterns of the dark liquid, and thought about all the blood that had been spilled. She'd been at the center of something monumental. Her whole world had shifted. In that quiet landscape, somewhere between the trees, she had been at the very core of the biggest massacre she had ever heard of. Gravity had shifted. The very Earth had shaken. And yet, nothing had happened. No one would ever know.

Tamanna took a deep breath. "Why did you tell me all of this?"

Romero started. He too, had been quietly pondering. He answered, "I told you, Ar—"

"No, I mean, why are you telling me this? Why would you tell me all of this, this classified information, just because Armand told you to? You're the boss, aren't you, not him?"

Romero's jaw shifted.

"Also," Tamanna continued, trying to stop her voice from getting too loud, "You said you made him get psycho hypnosis?

Why would you do that? If a captain sees an officer struggling, he suggests therapy or another line of career.

Why do you care that much about his actions and his words? Why is he so important?"

Romero's eyes turned sad. His gaze flitted from her eyes to a space just past her ear. "He… He's twenty-three years old. My son would have been twenty-three, too." he smiled again, humorlessly. "Armand lost his father when he was eleven. I lost my son when he was eleven. I found out when I received his admission files. The two incidents took place three months apart."

Tamanna shrank back into her seat. She didn't know how to express her condolences. Saying sorry sounded dumb. She had nothing to be sorry for, except for, perhaps, pressing on the subject. She couldn't be sorry. So, she let the silence fill the air. She sent the man, the big, important man, a meek little smile.

"I like all your cool badges."

The statement seemed to take him by surprise. Captain Dwight Romero smiled.

"Thanks, kid."

Then she took a deep breath. "I think I've been helping you a lot, right? I'll be a real help to the investigation, won't I?"

Romero smiled oddly. "Well, yeah. Why?"

"As a… *gift*, for being useful," Tamanna said hesitantly, feeling her fingers automatically meet and fiddle, "do you think…"

"Yeah?"

"I need a favor."

TWO WEEKS LATER

*H*i. *It's been a while, I'm sorry. There's been so much happening. I think its time I deserve to give you an update.*

The driver tinkered with the engine on purpose to stop it, then abandoned us on the side of the road so that George Torres could be murdered by Ilays Mehmoud Assaf as revenge. I still can't believe she'd do something like that. Thinking about everything that's happened, now, I think she isn't like the rest of them, right? They're all killers. Ilays is a killer too, but she isn't a murderer like them. She's a hero, to me at least.

Anyway, turns out George killed a colleague and then killed Theresia, Eden and Walter. That's what the reports say, anyway. I guess it's possible for a man as hunky as him to be able to rip out a woman's jaw, and stab a man twenty-something time. The reports also say Evangeline was an organ thief, and Ilays was her victim. They also say Ilays is a killer, but apparently, she's done things before, too, not just causing the death of that director. She listens to her readers and takes action. So, her family was given compensation money instead, and Ilays was never charged.

The funny thing is, they gave the Assaf family a LOT of compensation money. The reason why they gave so much isn't just because she did so much good, but because they also never found her body.

I told Evangeline she was getting old.

I still have her number. For some reason I keep texting, and I pretend I get a reply. It's always something witty and knowing. Sometimes I pretend she's fled the country to achieve greatness somewhere else. Sometimes I pretend she's camping right there in the forest where it all happened, and she's just waiting for me to return. I don't know. That's kind of stupid.

That brings me to Evangeline. So, she was charged as her former identity before the dementia, as Joanna-Marie Blocker, and arrested as an organ thief, and her past deeds have come to life. She came in the newspapers a few days ago. I read the paper today, and I know now that she was on her way, being taken to prison, ready to be put on trial, when the car she was in was stopped by a lone gunman.

The man did what he did and escaped, and when officers found the police van, the three escorting officials and Evangeline were all found dead. No one ever caught the shooter.

I've been riding the bus with Evangeline for six months now. She's smiled at me every day. She called me dear and I called her ma'am. She thought I was a good kid because I wrote in you, in a book with a pen and pencil. Speaking of, I almost lost you.

I told the police about Evangeline, which is (at least, I like to think) how they got so much information on her. I went to the station the day after Armand got into the accident and told them about the book, mine and Ilays's 'investigation', and how we all decided to escape together, and what Evangeline did in the end and how I thwarted her. I think Captain Romero is impressed. At the end of the interview, he said 'good job' and reminded me of the favor I asked. I received it.

Today morning, the official Party Bus incident was released to the newspapers. My parents read it. They read of the eight people on the party bus - the cop, the old woman, the gym coach, the salesman, the journalist, the cannibal, the model, and the child killer. Tamanna Raghavan was never on the bus. I was on a different bus the entire time. Because the school notified them that I never arrived, the bus never actually took me there. It went around in circles, confused. I hopped off at the intersection to get myself a coffee, and right when I was about to call my parents and tell them to pick me up, I saw a car crash. I had to go to the police the next day as a witness. The only connection I ever had to the pink party bus was that the man I saw get hit by a car was the officer who uncovered the ring of killers. My parents were worried sick, but Romero insisted — with a smile— that I did the right thing. He gave me a hundred dollars too, for some reason (and I wasn't about to refuse) and now all is well again.

Now, the driver was put on trial. He's going to jail. His bus didn't do anything wrong, so after it fulfilled its role as the crime scene, it was abandoned in a lot. George Torres came out of his coma yesterday, and he's going on trial soon. Isn't that ironic? The whole point of that journey was so that Ilays could find Gared's evidence, and she didn't. The only reason any of this happened was because George was supposed to die. Gared Mandela never cared about anyone else. In the end, everyone died— mostly— but George was the only one left living. At least he'll be going to jail, probably. But from what Romero tells me, George killed one innocent man, one dangerous man, and two literal murderers. So he's likely to have his sentenced reduced, or get the ability to go out on parole or something. I'm not too sure how it works.

Speaking of things working, Armand woke up from his coma yesterday, too. I'm going to visit him now. Mr. Romero invited me to. He says he wants Armand to quit his job and find something more mundane. I don't know how Armand will feel about that. Mr. Romero and I have been talking a lot this week, and from what I can tell, Armand is out of place in the police force anyway. He only got promoted to detective after the hypnopsychosis or whatever, because he accidentally uncovered some drug ring. Something like that. The heads of the ring ended up being his uncle and aunt, the very ones that abused him. Isn't that ironic too? Either way, I think the career change will be good for him. I can't wait to tell him about the Evangeline mystery.

—someone pushed her, and Tamanna looked up. A man apologized blandly and walked away. Tamanna slipped her phone into her pocket, wrapped her hands around herself, and walked briskly down the sidewalk. She slipped between two buildings and appeared at a public parking lot, divided from the alley by a steel link fence. Only when she was about to turn the corner again, and disappear into the traffic of pedestrians, did she turn and look for a single moment.

In the parking lot was a flamingo, in a sea of white, gray, silver and black buses. The writing on it was faded. The seats were empty.

It was a pink bus.

Tamanna turned, and walked away.

www.ingramcontent.com/pod-product-compliance
Lightning Source LLC
LaVergne TN
LVHW040004200726
843493LV00005B/1115